To L

Shuttered Seductions

Felicity Talisman

Original Version 2015

ISBN 978-17386583-9-8 (Paperback)

Prelude

“Okay, one thing he is, is a son-of-a-bitch,” Julia-Rae swore as she popped the lens cap off one of her two 35mm digital cameras and stared at the obscene crack running crookedly the lens. The camera was useless to her now. Her cheeks burned with rage as she flung her camera over her shoulder and stormed down the trail. “Lack of oxygen or not at this altitude, I’ll be damned. No man is going to bowl me over, disturb my shots, wreck my camera and take off without at least a decent apology. Mr. Name or no name magnificent tight cheeks, has a few things coming his way.” Julia-Rae yanked her sleeves up. “Oh, I’m so and so and I’m so sorry I’ve bowled you over. Here let me offer you a hand up; it’s the least I can do for you. MEN!” She fumed.

That insidious temper that had got her into so much trouble in the past sank its long, evil claws into her again. As her dad, Dennis McNaughton, would often tell her, “God didn’t plant that wavy pile of red hair on your head to act as traffic lights."

"You maybe the sexiest man I've seen in a long time, but you aren't getting away with this." The fire that gripped her heart now had also served her well in the past. It had gotten Julie-Rae through many trials and helped her to stay in command of her life. Of course, it had gotten her in a whole heap of trouble.

Turning a corner of the trail Julia-Rae spied the culprit crouched over staring at something on the stonewall foundations of the ancient city of Machu Picchu. She untied her handkerchief, twirled it taunt and held it like a slingshot. "Here Mr. Magnificent Great Ass, let's see how you like this!"

THWAP

Chapter One

Only an hour earlier Julia-Rae had staggered backwards and fell on her rear-end. Her camera gear clinked and clattered beside her over the rocky ground. A small cloud of fine dust swirled too easily upward in this land of little oxygen called Machu Picchu, Peru. Julia-Rae blinked trying to clear her vision as she looked upward and through a haze of little oxygen and stars a rough hand appeared. A man with dirty blonde curls of hair, camera equipment worn like long necklace bangles and a scruffy Peruvian smock stood before her. Obviously the fellow who had bowled her over; there wasn't anyone else on the thin ribbon of trail, that wound its way along the edge of the vertical mountain overlooking Machu Picchu.

"You, OK?" He muttered as he reached over and grabbed Julia-Rae's hand, pulling her effortlessly to her feet like a feeble ragdoll.

"You —cough— nearly slammed me into these rocks, or worse, you could have shoved me over the edge," Julia-Rae sputtered. A shudder ran through her at the thought of falling headlong into the rocks below. They were on a thin ledge of a trail, hundreds of feet below lay a jumble of jagged rocks, the Rio Vilcanota River winding through steep canyons and certain death.

"Yeah, I know, but isn't this place just so overwhelming." He spun away, seemingly losing interest in her. "Incredible. Don't you agree? Only discovered in 1911, built by whom and when no one really knows. Oh, they say it was the Incas, but no one is positive. I think only aliens could have lived up at this altitude and conceived all of this away from the prying eyes of humanity. Wow, truly a real modern day mystery."

He was truly a nutter, she thought. And I was alone with him.

On the edge, although more literally than she liked, but that was what she was trying to portray for the article in her fashion/adventure magazine magazine; The Edge For Today's Modern Woman. She came here looking for the ancient remains of man's intrusion into this hostile environment, besides the ruins of Machu Picchu, which could still be seen all around them. Terraces cut into the flanks of the virtually vertical mountain raced down to vanish into thin mists of fog. Mists that reminded Julia-Rae of the veils of a wedding dress. That was the image she was trying to get. At least, that was her focus until she had been bowled over by this strange man. Although a rather delicious looking man, she thought, staring into the handsome face with the square cut jaw. His blue eyes were surrounded by a sea of darkness, lending a hidden, reserved, almost dangerous look. God, he could take me anytime if he wanted, she mused.

What if he had a dozen unknown diseases, she laughed to herself. Better off to make friendly with the natives then, who probably hadn't heard of the invention of rubber, she supposed. Even though he had nearly done her in, Julia-Rae extended her hand in greeting and smiled politely trying to look like a visiting tourist.

"Machu Picchu!" He looked at her hand and spun away laughing, with the confident gait of a jungle cat.

Yup, mixed nuthouse galore with cashews thrown in. Half-mesmerized, Julia-Rae studied him as he disappeared around a bend in the trail. The solid cords of his leg muscles flexed as he walked and peeking out from behind the edges of the smock, the contours of a well-defined rear strained against the material of his worn jeans. God, he looked as good going, as he did coming. The man obviously worked out a lot or was born with a great rear.

With her hand still extended and her voice lost to the dizzying Andean slopes Julia-Rae said, “Hi, I’m Julia-Rae, go ahead and jump on me, everyone else does. You are. . .?”

Dust settled around her hikers as the imagined echoes of long dead Inca chiefs, chanting to strange, feathered gods resounded in her ears. Julia-Rae slowly withdrew her extended hand. So much for being nice to the locals.

“Well, he was magnificent. Rude, but magnificent.” Julia-Rae recalled the moment she had first laid eyes on the handsome stranger. She was sitting on the rocky ridge waiting patiently, for just the right amount of sun to steal through the clouds. She had come to learn over the years as a photographer that an exceptional picture sometimes took much perseverance.

The sudden constant sound of a camera’s shutter whirling with the annoyance of a cloud of mosquitoes, is what had disturbed her in the first place. It was coming from a person somewhere on the ridge just above her. Because of the steep angle she couldn't see who was up there. Finally Julia-Rae caught sight of a shadowy figure. She had been expecting to see some gaudy tourist sporting a disposable Kodak or packing an Apple phone or most likely some Android version of a Smartphone. While the man above her did fit the image of a tourist quite well, with his tattered Peruvian smock and worn blue jean pants, the three cameras, she could tell, were far from being Iphones or even expensive digitals.

What really struck her though, was his graceful fluidity as he moved around on the rocky outcrop above her. He balanced perfectly, the three cameras that slung from his shoulders. From her experience as a photographer Julia-Rae knew he had done this many times before. Moving with the taunt-coiled energy of a mountain lion, in perfect control of himself and his environment. He didn't just belong on that ridge, he stalked it like he owned it, dancing from boulder to boulder. For a pest he was sure striking, she thought.

His hair (longer than Julia-Rae cared for) was a scruffy, tawny blonde that streamed away from his face in loose, reckless abandon.

Yup, hair that just begged her to run her fingers through it as he lay on top of me. The rest of his face bore that Robert Redford look, with the thick jaw, brooding eyes and tight lips. Covering all of him was a blanket of tan, just dark enough to match the muscular hews of some fierce tribal warrior. A face, she imagined, that had spent much time being exposed to the sun in lands that bore mysterious, exotic names and where the nights brought no escape from the damnable heat. Lands where a person slept naked at night, with only a thin bedcover over them, or no cover at all. The thought of him naked next to her sent an erotic shiver through her. Keep your mind on your work, girl.

As he finally lifted his head from the camera, Julia-Rae caught a glimpse of what really lay beneath those brooding eyes. Up to this point she was certain he hadn't seen her. Being a photographer often meant being an observer, a voyeur in some respects. He was definitely attractive enough to enjoy watching. His eyes, like the stare of a jungle feline, seemed to catch everything, including her. Every movement, every nuance in every subtle shift of light, he caught it all and captured it, leaving not one conceivable angle unexposed to his camera. He was definitely another pro on assignment like herself. It was all Julia-Rae could do but not watch this man that moved with such purpose, strength and masculine grace.

She brushed at the dust clinging to her clothes. He could pounce like a cougar too. He had leapt down from that rocky ledge, bouncing from one outcropping of rock to another working his way down to the trail, until she realized too late that he would land on top of her.

"Well girl, you've done enough fantasizing. Heaven knows you can't afford to come to Peru twice." Still the thought struck her, as she unslung one of her cameras from around her neck. He'd make some fine pictures for the cover of a male pinup calendar or better yet, the cover of a romance novel. Or even better than that, him holding her in his arms, on the cover of that romance novel. She stared in shock at the camera as she popped the protective cover off.

About two minutes later

"Here Mr. Magnificent Great Ass, let's see how you like this!"

THWAP

"Yow-w!" The man, a complete stranger she had not ever met until a few moments ago yelled and spun around with astonishing speed, "what in th . . ."

Fury burned in his eyes as he locked onto the sight of Julia-Rae, standing there with the handkerchief dangling from her right hand with the I-shouldn't-have-done-that look on her face. For seconds neither spoke. Then, for the first time in her life, Julia-Rae felt her fury melting away like the coldest pack ice before the indomitable gates of Hell. Never, until now, had she met anyone with a passion and fury burning inside like he had great secrets locked into soul that could never be revealed. A thought chilled her, what if he was a sadistic, merciless killer or worse some sort of psycho rapist? What if he was to take her, here and now?

All sorts of wild thoughts ran through her head as he grabbed Julia-Rae by the shoulders and pinned her up against the cold stonewall. His strength was incredible, she was no match physically compared to him as he held her in a grip of steel. She was helpless, completely at his mercy. Yet the feeling of his hard callused hands sent a thrill through her. A strong scent assailed her nose. Hints of masculine cologne mixed with baser more elemental odors of sweat.

The aromas she hadn't realized could be so; so arousing.

It had been a long while since she had been in a man's arms. They were alone and he could do virtually anything he wanted with her. What had I done? Damn temper of mine.

"Get your hands off me," Julia-Rae implored weakly. The strength of her anger had deserted her. She was not at all like the strong, full of inner fury person that had raged only moments before. The weakness in her voice shocked her. Her strength, her anger, had deserted her, she didn't realize how weak she sounded without it. This was not the Julia-Rae she knew, had ever known. The in-control-of-her-destiny woman who ran her own magazine company. Pulling from that earlier rage she spoke again, demanding, as she wanted to originally say, "get your hands off me." No, it was as if he was looking in amusement at her. Maybe he had never met a woman who held her ground. Maybe he just like toying with his women, like a cat with a trapped mouse.

She should be terrified, she had placed herself in mortal danger. He could do anything he wanted with her, yet there was something comforting and reassuring in the strength of his hands and in his gaze. He simply stared with those eyes of the most intense blue she had ever seen. Eyes that seethed with passion and fury. Julia-Rae swallowed and drew again from her inner fury, pulling some of her anger back to herself. “You’ve got some nerve bowling me over. Wrecking one of my cameras and not having the decency to even introduce yourself or even stop to see if I’ve been injured,” she blurted, trying to keep that rage fueled. This was the Julia-Rae she had known all her life, headstrong and feisty. But how could anyone stay angry when they stared into eyes like his?

“And you’ve some temper.” His hands lightly traveled down her arms, almost caressing her, as if she were an ornament to be admired, as he released her. Bastard. His eyes never left hers. Julia-

Rae sensed those eyes were sizing her up, studying everything about her. He moved slightly back, barely giving them breathing space.

She tried to not let her response to that casual caress, from his rough hands show, but something in his eyes told her he caught that shiver of arousal, the slight intake of breath, the nearly inaudible sigh and the fury. The fury of being treated as an object on display. Julia-Rae had fought all of her life to be more than that. Of course, it had gotten her in a whole heap of trouble, much to the dismay of her father, in her younger days. Everything from Julia-Rae telling the next door neighbor where to go, to the time she nearly scratched the eyes out of the first boy who tried to kiss her when she was twelve.

Sometimes she wished she could be just some dumpy girl with ordinary brown hair instead of being the full figured woman with the head of wild curly red hair that made most men look at her like she was a daydream out of an adult magazine. Although she was dressed in loose fitting jogging clothes, a heavy sweater and a Goretex raincoat, he'd never know what she really looked like under that getup. Now that she thought about it she often dressed down just so that men wouldn't ogle over her. This was the first time in her life she had become conscious of how much she hated being treated like an object of adoration.

"Who wouldn't be upset when some stranger bowls them over, takes off without a thought to see if they're okay, a proper introduction and not even an offer to pay for clothes you've sullied." Julia-Rae spat out before realizing what she had said. Maybe it was the quiver on those tight lips, lips surrounded by a growth of stubble, from a couple of days of lack of shaving. Lips that were so close she could reach over and kiss them. What was she thinking?

If he was a true gentleman, he'd taken a step or two back after he released her and not stand virtually nose to nose, breathing on her.

He was a complete stranger and she was here on an assignment, not trying to find a romantic encounter on a foreign mountaintop. Mind you the idea seemed quite enticing and arousing. Not to mention he smelled so darn good.

"Sullied? Sullied," he said tasting the word, smacking his lips as a connoisseur would before sampling a sumptuous dish, savoring each syllable like the aromas wafting from the food. "Now that is an interesting and most unusual word. I like it." An impish grin lit his face. "Sullied, Madame, I'm truly sorry but it appears that I've sullied your clothes. I'll have Burtrum the butler take them to the drycleaners," he mimicked in a high well to do British accent.

That bastard, her eyes blazed as fury gripped her heart. Julia-Rae raised her hand. Almost instantly rationality screamed at her senses to stop. What was she about to do? He could break her neck in a second if he chose to or do even worse things to her.

He looked unflustered as he quickly grabbed her hand, pinned it against her side and roughly pressed her up against the cold stonewall again. This time he shoved himself against her, pressing her to the stone with his body. The hardness of his muscular chest crushed her breasts, flattening Julia-Rae to the unyielding rock. The thump of heat from his crotch rubbing against her.

She had nearly slapped a stranger. Concern for her safety ran through her. He had the strength to do with her whatever he wished. There were only a dozen or so other tourists scattered among these ruins. As he inhaled his chest moved against her breasts. Her nipples, unburdened by a bra, hardened at the sensation. The silent glint in his eyes let her know that he was enjoying this as much as her. His groin crushed against hers. Hard rock pressed her from behind, yet not as hard as the man pinning her.

He said nothing as he stared at her, with those eyes of the deepest blue intensity. Julia-Rae could have sworn his eyes were on fire, a deep blue azure fire of passion. With those eyes he smiled at her, either from enjoying her helplessness or the sensation of her pressed up against him, she didn't know which. Or maybe from amusement? Why did he elicit such raging emotion from her? His lips were only an inch from hers, looking so kissable with moisture gleaming on them. From deep down inside came the cry, kiss me. Kiss me, now. How long ago had it been since she had desired a man to kiss her? Julia-Rae swallowed, choking down the desire, or do more with her and she'd be helpless under his domination?

"You can unhand me at any time," she gasped, Julia-Rae was not about to apologize for her actions, it would only show she was weak. Although she realized it might be the more prudent course of action to take.

Still, he remained silent, studying her like a lion would, deciding if he should devour his prey or merely torture it some more. No, his eyes weren't merely smiling at her there was much more there. It was as if they were surprised by her antics. What had made her say sullied? Julia-Rae's mother died at her birth and she had been raised by her very English grandmother. She would often read Julia-Rae stories of English romance and some of the strange, antiquated words they used she would sometimes repeat while playing as a child.

“I admire a woman of passion and it appears the fire that marks your hair has extended to your lips. While those lips say release me, your eyes tell a different tale. A surrendering tale of take me, here and now. I like it.” He wouldn’t, would he? What if he decided to have her, here and now? A throb from inside answered her. The man merely sneered and slowly released his strong grip on her and backed away.

“But being a gentleman, I wouldn’t do that. Here.” He said hard emphasis on the last word.

The sudden coolness sent a shudder through her as Julia-Rae struggled to keep herself up on legs that had turned to rubber long ago. As much as she didn’t want to admit, she was disappointed that he had released her. There was one part of her that rather enjoyed having him pressed up against her. To be that near a stranger, to feel the beat of his heart against her chest. The heat from his lips. The unmistakable throb of his maleness, wanting her, calling to her. What would he be like driving into me? Taking me? Some part deep, deep inside moaned.

"You have my apologies. If I've dirtied your clothes and damaged the lens to your camera then I'll repay you," he said as he unslung one of his cameras. "Roy Sutter and since there is only one train ride back down this mountain, I'm sure we'll both be on it. If you don't mind I'd like to at least buy you supper tonight, when we get back down."

"I'm Julia-Rae McNaughton and I think that is the least you could do besides offering me the use of one of your cameras, as a way of making up for the inconvenience."

"Well, the thought had crossed my mind, except I've already got rolls of film on the go in all of the cameras and I don't imagine you use the old fashioned 35mm single reflex like I do. So after I finish one of these rolls then you're welcome to use my camera and supper is still offered to you. Unless of course you just want my digital instead?"

"Offer accepted." She could tell he was about to say something inane like if you know how to use the darn thing. She'd grown up on the devices, long before digital took over the film world.

"Good, it's the least I can do. But right now, like you, I have to get back to my picture taking, we've only got a couple of hours left before leaving. Meet me on top of that platform of rock in a few minutes, I'll wait for you up there, when the sun comes out from the clouds shortly we'll get a few great pictures of the valley below as the shadows lengthen across it." With that he sauntered off already lost in a world of lighting angles and camera close ups, a world Julia-Rae had to also rejoin.

Julia-Rae watched him walk slowly away. He had the air of a reporter, but there was something different about him.

His hand absently rubbed at the spot she had twapped with her bandanna as he disappeared around the corner of a building. “Serves him right,” Julia-Rae giggled. “Men, always get ya into trouble dearie,” her granny would often say. Julia-Rae straightened out her outfit, turned and walked back along the trail she had stormed down earlier. Enough of the distractions she had some serious work to do. But God, he felt good pressed up against her.

“Where did the man get his energy from?” Julia-Rae wheezed as she stared up at the daunting stone staircase before her. He had bounded up to the platform he had pointed to earlier as if he were a mountain goat with his own built in oxygen tank, which some people needed up here at these extreme altitudes. There had to be a good fifty stone cut stairs still in front of her yet to go. How the hell did the natives manage to build this place, she gasped.

“Hurry or you’ll miss some of the best shots.” His voice called down from somewhere above her.

Taking several deep breaths of the cool mountain air Julia-Rae continued her ascent. “Damn this altitude,” she muttered hoarsely, her heart threatening to burst from her chest, yet there was no way she’d allow him to show her up. Still, each intake of air burned its way down her throat. Finally, the last step came into view; the back of each leg throbbed in agony. She had to rest for a moment. “Give me a chance to catch my breath.” Her throat burned raw in the high climate. “What I’d give for a good hot cup of tea about now.” She said announcing her presence to Roy as he moved about on the plateau.

“Actually, coffees better out here it helps to open the breathing passages. I’ve suffered from soroche only once before and it wasn’t a pretty sight.” “Soroche?”

“Native word for high altitude or mountain sickness.” Roy walked over to help Julia-Rae. “Or you could try what the natives use to invigorate themselves and open their breathing passages up. It's a mild hallucinogenic, called mate de coca made from a brew of coca leaves, kinda gives them a buzz." He smiled at her. "I'm glad you could make it."

Smug bastard were all men strung out on testosterone poisoning like him. "Yeah, me too, no wonder the natives look so happy around here and I thought it was the simple living. Didn't realize they were stoned, explains how they could work this high up, that or most likely to be chatting to the holy mother or whatever they believed in."

He shook his head, smile on his face, at her. "I've taken the last of the pictures on this roll and reloaded the camera, it's all yours. I'll just give you a few pointers."

Julia-Rae was still wheezing lightly as she set her equipment down, trying to get enough oxygen back into her lungs. Roy hadn't given her the chance to say that she'd handled dozens of cameras in her time as he strolled up from behind her. The warmth of his body, his sudden closeness caught any words in her throat. Cutting off all thought of saying anything. He felt like a security blanket thrown over her shoulders as he lifted his hands and placed the camera around her neck.

"The sun is about to split those clouds again and if my guess is right the effect of its rays spreading across the valley should be spectacular from our viewpoint. Now be a little patient with my old friend, he's a virgin. "What?"

"I've never let a woman touch him before."

"I hope not all your equipment's like that." Julia-Rae giggled and shook her head. This man was obviously demented from the altitude, or maybe that was his problem, permanent soroche overdose.

"Only the cameras, if that's what you mean." He said, sounding indignant. "My equipment has had its fair share of use. Now this guy is not a point and shoot, but if you follow his lead he'll take you to the best shots and angles." Roy slipped his arms through the inside of hers his hands grazed her body as they went by. Roy drew his self up close as he raised the camera.

Julia-Rae hoped he wasn't a point and shoot type of guy, kinda put all the fun out of lovemaking. "Hey I. . ."

"Relax, I'm not trying to feel you up, just trying to show you how to operate the controls. Although I will say nice body. I do like my women with curves."

The sudden warmth of his body pulled at Julia-Rae senses. Her breath caught in her throat, she wanted to push him away, yet didn't. His hands ran down her sides. The sheer audacity and exhilarating domination of a man in charge. She quivered, would he?

"For this brightness, I keep the F-stop where it is and you'll have to focus constantly, like so." His arms tightened around her as he reached for the focus slider on the camera. His heat entered her from behind. She just wanted to close her eyes, moan and let him take control.

"I think I've done this once or several hundred times, thank you." She knew all the controls like taking a walk down the old streets in her hometown. Her legs already wobbly from the climb up began to turn to the consistency of Jell-O and the stability of wet spaghetti as his strong arms closed around her. A tremble ran through her as some long-forgotten seed of desire sprouted inside. Was this guy some expert at seduction or was this just her long-suppressed craving for affection springing to life? Julia-Rae shook her head, lifted the camera from his fingers and stepped forward, breaking the closeness and the spell of his warmth. If she didn't in another second, she knew she'd collapse into his arms and beg him to have his way with her. God, he felt so damn good and strong. "Thanks for the pointer, now we must hurry before our train ride back departs and it is a long climb back down."

“You’re right, sure enough.” He smiled, looking for all the world like some hungered alley cat that had come across a fresh fish in a garbage can.

And this one is not going to be is easy meat, buster.

At that precise moment the sun split the clouds and lit the whole city spread out below them with brilliant rays of sunlight. The effect of the sunbursts, running down through the shifting clouds, in a constant movement on the grey of the rock walls was splendorous.

Damn, she had begun to dislike him for being right all the time. Roy had indeed picked out the perfect vantage point to take pictures. Julia-Rae began to focus and shoot, lost in marveling at the rays of sunlight dancing back and forth across the gray rock like angels cast in stop motion lighting with all the glories of heaven. She’d momentarily forgotten about Roy, until incessant clicking reminded her he was snapping away taking pictures of his own. Only when Julia-

Rae turned around did she realize that he was taking more pictures of her than the valley below.

"Say cheese and hold that pose." The wind had gently lifted her hair and Julia-Rae could feel the flush of sunlight on her cheeks as the sun finally spread its light across the platform. Julia-Rae stood transfixed on the ledge with the sun's brilliant light streaming across the plateau beneath them. The city walls of Machu Picchu highlighted in various shades. She closed her eyes and lifted her head, soaking up the warming rays for the briefest of moments. It reminded her of being a young girl again, for this was something she always did as a child. She felt like an old tomcat lying lazily before a huge picture window, luxuriating in the suns warmth.

"Perfect. I'll send you a copy." He said before returning to continue his voracious picture taking. His words broke the spell cast ever so briefly by the sun and Julia-Rae opened her eyes. She watched him silently as man, camera and environment blended into one. His eyes caught the subtlest of views, the slightest nuances of angles. It was like watching a ballet dancer in slow motion, twisting, turning with his gear, all the while taking pictures. He had been wonderful to watch from a distance, mesmerizing to see in action this close. Julia-Rae raised her camera and snapped off three pictures of Roy before he noticed. He simply smiled and kept clicking away.

Okay girl, back to work. She told herself and turned to her task of taking pictures of the plain and its mystical ruins, highlighted by the energy of the sun.

“Well, shall we start heading back for the train?” Roy spoke breaking the silence cast by the beguiling whistle of mountain wind and the crispness of the altitude.

She glanced at her watch. “Yeah it’s about that time.” Julia-Rae unslung her camera from around her neck and with a well rehearsed move rewound the film, popped open the back of the camera. She grabbed an unused roll of her own film and deftly loaded the new roll into his camera.

Roy stood with mouth agape.

"Thanks for the use of your camera and you're right I've used one of these Nikon D800's in the past. They are a trusty friend to have in the biz."

His mouth hadn't shut yet. "I'm sorry, I guess I. . .a"

"Shouldn't presume I'm a helpless female."

"I can see that now."

"Like you, I'm a professional photographer and I used to own one on those Nikons a few years ago."

"Well, I guess since we're riding back down on this train together we'll have something to talk about then."

"Who said I wanted company?"

Roy bent down onto one knee as if he was about to propose to her. He gently grabbed her left hand. "This over presuming gentleman requests the company of the distinguished lady in his presence to join him in discussion of various matters, personal sentiments and business arrangements, will she accept his humble offer of his delightful company."

Julia-Rae giggled, the touch of his hands weren't only warm and exhilarating, they were familiar. His breath washed over the surface of her skin like the spray of jasmine and patchouli flowers at night; exciting and stimulating. "Okay, okay, get off your knees please, you're just getting dirty."

"Ah, thank you for the honor." He pulled her hand to his lips and gently kissed it before rising. Julia-Rae shuddered as the feeling of deja-vu swept over her again. It was as if she'd been kissed that very way, a thousand times before in the past, in some forgotten era of chivalry. By him. Shivers ran through her as he stood up and she stared into his face, into those incredible blue eyes. Eyes that spoke of hunger and desire, knowing that she was the igniting force, she was the tender morsel roasting on the spit before him. The warm wetness of his lips, their hunger against her flesh.

"Yes," she said, the sarcasm evaporated and in a softer more sincere tone added, "but let me do some writing first. I need to collect my thoughts on the pictures I took here and put it into words while it's still fresh in my mind." Which was nothing, Julia-Rae pondered, compared to the thoughts she was having of him.

"Sure, I do the same after each photographic expedition. I'll meet you on the train, I want to go over to the back side of the city first and I'll be quick." He glanced at his watch.

"Okay, I'll stay here and catch my breath before I head back, I've got enough pictures for what I need. And there's no way I can go walking anymore."

They gathered their equipment, and as they did Julia-Rae knew somewhere in her heart he had broken past that first barrier. With that touch he'd already wormed his way into her soul and opened some locked door. She watched him recede down the stairs, his blonde hair swept back by the ever-constant mountain breeze was the last thing she saw and of course that rear she wouldn't mind cupping in her hands someday. Preferably on top of her. Christ girl, get a bloody grip.

The click, clack of the train, its constant sway and the snort of the steam emanating from its engine all settled around Julia-Rae as she wrote down her notes. Voices from the other passengers seemed to blend into the cacophony of sounds being emitted by the steam powered train that traveled these tracks. Even the greenery of the jungle whizzing by didn't disturb her as she jotted down her notes, trying to capture everything while it was still fresh in her mind. Machu Picchu was as adventurous a place as one could ever hope to find, even more so. Or maybe it was Roy, perhaps he'd awoken some long-stilled voice.

The crunch of the seat beside her alerted her that someone had settled into it. She didn't have to look up to know it was Roy. The tingles that ranged up her arm told her that. His presence seemed reassuring, almost comforting and exciting at the same time.

"Hey, I'm done jotting down my notes, how about you." His voice belayed his excitement.

"Yes pretty much."

"Good, I've arranged a surprise, come with me."

Julia-Rae barely had time to nod yes before Roy grabbed her hand and yanked her upright. "Where are. . ."

"Shhh, I'll show you something special."

He pulled her to the back of the train car, which was the last one before the caboose.

"What are you?"

Roy flung open the heavy door just as the train's whistle sounded. Julia-Rae jumped with a start. Her heart hammered away. She had to catch her breath in the chill of the air. They were outside the train car and before her was about a two foot wide platform. Roy pushed her to one side and edged beside her closing the door behind them. The caboose's platform was about two feet away, between the two hurtled only empty space and rail ties below whizzing by dizzily. The fresh scented jungle tore by on either side in ever changing shades of green.

"Are you absolutely out of your mind?" She screamed over the noises generated by the train as it hurtled down the Andean mountain.

"Yes, I do believe that is correct," he spoke in an English well to do accent. "Now, just follow me and don't look down." He jumped to the other platform.

"Not a frigging chance." Julia-Rae stood there her knuckles white clinging to the railing. She knew all the color had drained from her face as she stared at the blur of ties and the train's buckle that clunked back and forth in its grip holding the two cars together. The railing suddenly seemed to turn to jelly in her hands. Knees threatening to turn to tapioca.

“I said don’t look down!” He hollered.

“Then next time don’t mention it or just tell me to look you in the eyes.”

“What and see my cataracts. Don’t think so. Come on red, I’ll catch you.”

Julia-Rae swallowed hard. I hope he’s as real a man as he looks. I don’t even have time to say good-bye, cruel world or call my granny. She jumped in time to the jostling of the train cars.

Why couldn’t I have stayed in my seat? Yet inside that spark of the mischievous ten-year-old girl smiled with glee, the one that loved being on the edge of excitement and danger. She was still shrieking as Roy caught her. Her friend Linda had once told her the emotions of fear and excitement is the same, it’s just a matter of how a person interprets the emotion. So is ecstatically overjoyed the same deal as scared shitless?

Roy pulled her tight to him, the hardness of his body, consoling her, gripping her. Perhaps Linda was right, it was all a matter of interpretation. For a brief moment he held her in his arms, staring down at her with those blue eyes of desire. Her heart hammering like a Big Ben clock gone mad. Her breasts crushed against him, nipples she knew were already hardened from the cold, now from the crush of his maleness. This man was sheer exhilarating take-meto-the-edge-of-my-comfort-zone lunacy. She loved it.

"Okay, that was the hard part. Now follow me." He let her go and opened the door to the caboose. Smells of old wood, coffee and dank staleness assailed her nose as she entered the dimly lit room. Judging by the haphazard mess of everything, boxes lay strewn about, papers hung in a profusion from the walls, it was easy to see this was an area passengers aren't normally allowed in; or anyone for that matter that been born with any kind of incentive for cleaning. He closed the door shutting out the noise and blur of jungle.

"Are you trying to kill me?" Julia-Rae spat as she spun around her temper flaring to life. "Or just trying to scare my soul out of my body? Or is this some sick way of getting revenge for that thwap on your ass?"

"Nah, if I wanted to do that I'd just have pushed you from the train. Did I ever tell you, you're awfully sexy when the fire in your eyes matches your hair?"

Julia-Rae stood there biting her lip, fighting back the anger until she realized the silliness of her situation and then burst into laughter. "God, that was exhilarating!" She uttered, allowing truth to speak its rare voice from her heart.

"It sure was, now follow me."

As they both turned an older Spanish looking fellow bearing a railroad uniform, came walking towards them. "Hi senor, I see you bring the senorita to catch the view." He said in good English as he held out his hand. Roy pulled out a wad of money from his pocket and slipped him some bills in US currency. The gentlemen stepped aside to let them pass.

"Did you just bribe that man to let us pass?"

"Yup, the almighty payoff, I've learned years ago that in some countries the only way to get what you want or get any kind of service, is to pay a little extra."

"Pay extra for what?"

"For this." Roy opened the last door to the caboose and they walked outside standing on the back platform of the caboose.

Jungle whisked by on both sides. Overhead the clear of the mountain sky with its vivid stark deep blue hues beckoned. Through peeks in the jungle she could see across the valley to the impressive array of neighboring peaks and lush green valleys.

"I realize you can see much of the same view from your seat. But you can't feel it or smell it like you can hear." He inhaled deeply. "Besides this is a bit more private."

"That it is." Julia-Rae said as she tilted her head back and with one hand brushed her profusion of red curly hair back. She reveled in the sun's warm magic as it caressed her face. Overhead the morning mist had long since evaporated from the burned away by the strength of the mid-day sun. It promised to be a hot day, yet Julia-Rae enjoyed the coolness of the breeze generated by the train as it sped down the tracks.

"What a day it's been." He spoke breaking the silence.

"Yes, this was just the break I needed from work."

"Oh yeah, what exactly do you do?"

"I run a magazine called "The Edge for Today's Woman." It focuses on things like what a modern self-reliant woman of the twenty-first century does on her days off."

"Interesting, sounds like a tense job, so is this a holiday then?"

"Yes very intense and just last week I had another company make offers to buy me out. I think I'm stealing away their business or at least hope I am."

“Well, this is a good sign I suppose that you’re successful, but isn’t there other things in life that you’d sooner be doing?”

Julia-Rae was glad he didn’t say anything chauvinistic like raising kids or looking after a home. After today’s events she didn’t have the energy to get angry with him. “No, I guess running my own business is my life. Although I think I was a little bit harsh with the fellow that came to my office the other day.”

“Harsh, what do you mean?”

“I was having a bad day, sometimes the pressure of running my own business is too much I guess. It all started with a loud knock at my door.”

A knock that sounded louder and with more authority than Cindy usually rapped on the door.

“Come in.” Julia-Rae said as she looked up from her fingers and quickly dropped her hands back on her desk. He was an expected appointment.

A swarthy, well-dressed European looking gentleman walked into her office. He bore a briefcase, two piece Armani suit, swarthy complexion and a definite cultured attitude. She guessed Italian. “Ms. Julia-Rae McNaughton, I presume.”

Safe to say things just got worse. By his accent she guessed right, Italian. Hopefully not Mafia related, she chuckled to herself. “Yes?”

“I represent the Stanza group of magazines, I’m sure you’ve heard of them.”

She sure had; it was one of her main competitors.

“We are interested in your production called The Edge.”

“What do you mean interested?” She didn’t like the sounds of this fellow. He struck her as the type of individual that usually got what he wanted. His rather round face portrayed no smugness, just another day on the job to this fellow. If there was emotion in his soul, it didn’t show through his cold and calculated eyes.

"I won't waste much of your time or mine. Your magazine, The Edge, has been picked by the executive board of Stanza as one of the magazines we'd like to acquire. I have in my briefcase an initial proposal, do read it over, at your leisure and give me a call. If I haven't heard from you in say a couple of weeks, I'll give you a call."

Julia-Rae heard, through the grapevine, that their line of travel magazines were suffering in sales lately. She knew her last quarter sales results were good and had a hunch her magazine was responsible for a good part of Stanza's decline. So, what do the big boys say, 'If you can't beat the competition, buy them out.'

He calmly set his expensive briefcase on top of her desk. The briefcase fit the man, gold edged and wrapped in black, tight, uncompromising leather. She caught a whiff of the leather as he opened the case. Some of her papers slid off to one side and fell onto the floor. He pulled a large sheaf of papers from his case, not caring about hers. The papers were bound and set in an official folder. Someone had spent a lot of time putting this together. He handed them to her. Julia-Rae stared in disbelief at the cover letter. Julia-Rae quickly scanned over the document. It looked basically like a buy-out scheme, keeping her on as the president, yet answering to Stanza Corporation board of directors, on any final decisions. She read the bottom line and what they were willing to pay her was close to what she had already invested. Inside the pot, that brewed her nasty temper, began a quick boil. One thing she really disliked in life was having men think they can push her around just because she was female. This Euro type fellow Mr. didn't even give me his name, walk in, toss my papers on the ground, not offer to pick them up and take over my company. Smoke was curling out of her ears. He would have no scruples pushing her or most anyone else for that matter around.

"Do you have any questions at this time?"

"Just one, Mr. Ah, I didn't quite catch your name."

“Antonio, Antonio Rofuko.” He rose and extended his hand. It was an automatic gesture. In fact everything about him seemed automatic.

Julia-Rae rose, “Get Out!” She had no patience for him or his pompous kind today, she had to get her next issue out and figure a way to get some Hong Kong pictures for that issue.

“Excuse me.” His hand remained extended into empty space unshaken.

He was cool alright.

A look of nervousness cracked its way across his cool demeanor. She had caught him, at least a little off guard; perhaps he wasn’t used to dealing with an abrupt, confident woman. Julia-Rae gave him credit, though, he recovered quickly. The man was very good at what he did. “We are open to negotiating certain parts of the agreement if they are not satisfactory.”

"Get out, before I have you thrown out." Julia-Rae knew the heat suffusing her face was turning her cheeks a crimson color. "I'm not sure on the polite office etiquette on a matter such as this so I won't go there. How about I just say this straight, business person to business person and get this through your head. We have no agreement. Never had and never will. I'm not interested in selling this business. Now remove your slimy presence from this office before it fouls the air and I need to send in the fumigators. Now, before I call the police."

Antonio slowly withdrew his hand and closed his briefcase. "Well I suppose I'll give you time to look over the proposal more in length. I'll give you a call, say next week?" He looked at her with a cold snaky stare.

"You, son of a . . ." His words did little to quell her tide of anger. Julia-Rae pressed her intercom. She had to get him out of the office before she really blew it and did something she'd regret. "Cindy, kindly escort Mr. Rofuko out of my office immediately."

Antonio turned and quietly left the office. She knew he was too much of a businessman than to get involved in anything as ugly as being evicted from the office. Yet his face bore an unmistakable, we're not quite finished dealing with each other just yet, look. "Oh and Cindy, screen the rest of my calls until lunch, thanks." She needed to get to work on her last project, but it was clear there were far were pressing matters to attend to, like what to do about the Hong Kong spread.

"And that is the skinny on why I decided to come here. My father always blamed my red hair for my razor sharp temper." "This I can attest too." Roy rubbed his rear.

Julia-Rae laughed. "Sorry. That's what I meant. I blew it with the lawyer I know. So I thought a good break to get away from it all and take some pictures would be great.

This is the part of the job I much more prefer, being out there."

"On The Edge, like the title of your magazine." He thought a moment, "so are you considering his offer?"

"Not really, I enjoy running my business and when I'm gone, I've got Cindy my secretary who I know I can trust to look after the place. She's like my right arm, runs the computers, refrags them and all that jazz. I don't know what I'd do without her or even if I could function."

"That's good, you've got someone reliable to run the ship while you're away. People like that are hard to find."

"I know." Just then they passed a clearing in the trees and Julia-Rae spotted a small boy leading his llama along a gravel road that crossed over the train tracks. Julia-Rae waved and the lad waved back. A warm smile on his tanned face. "I admire the people around here they seem to have so little in their lives and yet seem so happy overall."

"There are many countries I've visited and it seems to be that way in most poorer countries. I think all of our richness and material possessions only gives us more stress most of the time."

"Isn't that the truth?" Julia-Rae closed her eyes again, they were nearly back down the mountain. The heat of the sun warmed her face. Roy seemed so easy to talk to and at the same time he possessed that crazy put-me-on-the-edge-of-my-seat and not know what to expect exhilaration. The kind of man she often read about but never met. "You travel around lots then?"

"Yeah, being a freelance photographer, I'm often gone on assignment somewhere."

"Find it lonely?" She asked without thinking. The one thing she had noticed about him, no ring or marks to show where one had been.

"Yeah, I do sometimes, although I've come to realize years ago that my life style wasn't conducive to married life."

"Single then?"

"Yes."

"Yourself?"

"Yes."

Julia-Rae smiled as a shudder ran through her. He was single.

The conversation had taken an uncomfortable closeness. "I think I'd like to return to my seat now, getting a bit chilly."

As Roy turned to open the door to the caboose she stared up into his blue eyes. Eyes that spoke of passion and sensitivity and called to a part of her soul she had denied a long time ago. "Thanks for bringing me out here, it was incredible. Dangerous as hell, but incredible fun, thanks."

"My pleasure, are we still on for supper tonight?"

"Sure, meet me at the front lobby of my hotel, the Don Carlos, around 8:00."

"Deal, I'll bring a hearty appetite and I know a good restaurant, the Dos de Mayo. It serves Spanish as well as North American type meals."

"Sounds good to me. I don't mind trying other countries foods, normally, but after all of today's excitement, I think I'd like to stick with something familiar."

Just then the whistle of the train blew, jolting Julia-Rae. "Looks like we're back down, see you tonight."

The waiter escorted them to an intimate table near the back of the restaurant. It was cozy, had far too many plants, a candle at each table, sensuous latin music in the background and trouble. Romance and seduction hung in the air in cloying wisps; definitely trouble. Stay focused girl, she thought to herself. You've no time to be doing the all-night romance thing. Eat, drink, and be merry. She had a plane to catch and lots to prepare before taking off tomorrow. She didn't have time for the dessert, which if had his way would be him.

"Would you like to look at our wine list?" The tall Spanish looking waiter asked.

"Go ahead, Julia-Rae, I don't drink." "Oh, is that by choice?" She asked politely.

"Just, not my thing." He blurted.

His eyes bore a fleeting glimpse of pain as the words came out just a little too fast and with an undercurrent of a growl. Not wanting to wreck the mood she decided not to go there. Something to ask another time, if they ever got closer she decided. Another time, the thought hit her briefly. Would she like to see him again? A tingle ran through her in response. "I'll try a liter of your Merlot, thanks." If she was mousy, she'd have followed his example and done what was prudent and not ordered any wine. However, one thing Julia-Rae was never good at was being mousy.

She pulled out the card he had given her earlier on the train ride back down and stared at it. "So, according to your business card as you mentioned earlier, you're a freelance photographer," Julia-Rae smiled, "most interesting."

"And why is that?" Roy smiled back at her.

He was being very polite, not at all the devil may care, I don't, attitude he had up on the mountain. Then again, Julia-Rae thought, she kind liked that carefree almost boyish charm about him. Not to mention the passion that seemed to exude from him. It was so much like her own deep passion she put into producing her magazine. "Well, I didn't think you were a used car salesman."

"Oh, and what exactly does that mean? I've been known to off load a few Pontiacs and even the occasional Caddy." He raised his eyebrows obviously put off guard by her comment.

Julia-Rae's mind shot back to the scene on the ridge where she first saw Roy. "I was watching you on that ridge, the way you managed to balance the cameras and take all those shots. You never seemed to quit moving. Very fluid, a natural." What really caught her attention was the strong masculine grace and confidence he showed as he worked. It had not only caught her attention, but excited her. The erotic thought of his body moving with such sensual grace on top of her, naked, raced across her mind and tore at her rationality.

The menu slipped from Julia-Rae's fingers and she caught it before it crashed against the water glasses and made a mess. She was surprised at how nervous she was, just sitting here with this man. It wasn't just because he was good looking. It was more. There was an uneasiness sitting this close to him. Maybe it was that intense look in his eyes. Did he possess half the passion that seared inside those incredibly deep, dark wells? Maybe it was just her, she had been a long time without a man in her life. Five years to be exact, since Tim.

Images of that last date with Tim still haunted her, unexpectedly, at night. They were in his apartment. Tim had taken them out for dinner and had invited Julia-Rae up to his apartment, where he started coming on to her. She said no, but Time wasn't hearing that as an option. At one point he had pinned her to the floor and was tearing at her underclothes. If she hadn't smashed a vase against his head and ran from his place, she'd have become another statistic of date rape on a police report. A chill ran through her, at the recollection. I thought I could trust him, what a mistake.

"Care to order?" The waiter interrupted.

"Oh," Julia-Rae jumped slightly, disturbed from her earlier remembrances. She looked up and caught a momentary look of concern in his eyes. Eyes of such calm and at the same time such intense sensuous passion. It was hard not to slip into some sort of fantasy when she stared into them. She quickly glanced at the menu. "Yes, I'll have the Cuy, roast stuffed guinea pig and a Caesar salad to start."

"I'll order in a minute." Roy said. The waiter politely walked away. As Roy perused the menu, Julia-Rae looked around the restaurant. There were mainly only couples in the restaurant. Two tables down sat two people who looked like they were on their honeymoon. They had a bottle of wine at their table, were holding hands and staring into each other's eyes. A candle was lit, yet the glow at the table seemed to exude from them. The glow of young lovers. It had been a long time since Julia-Rae had been in love. She thought back to university where she had first met Tim. He seemed like a nice enough type of guy at the time. As it turned out not too damn pleasant. Pleasant enough to try to have his way with her, whether she wanted to make love or not. The funny thing was that if he'd had more patience with her she would have eagerly made love to him. Made love to him, had his babies and lived the life of a typical middle class housewife. Julia-Rae smiled at herself. Yeah, right, who was she to kid? The woman voted most likely to succeed. The woman that most men only admired from a distance, perhaps fantasized about but never asked out on a date. In fact she usually had to ask guys to get up and dance with her. Being headstrong, as her dad called her, had its advantages and its pitfalls.

"Caesar salad? I hear they use a lot of garlic here," Roy blurted out.

Julia-Rae snapped out of her reminiscing. "And your point is? I don't intend to kiss anyone tonight." Although she'd like to find out just how hot those tight lips of his would feel against hers. Kissing her lips, her neck and nibbling at her ears. A hot shudder raced through her, his lack of interest was somehow arousing. The cat playing mouse. What if she took control and took him to bed, mounted him. Oh, the wine is kicking in. If she kept this up she'd never make it through this meal.

"One never knows what can transpire during an evening."

It was the first time he had dropped any indication that he even was remotely interested in her. Although by the way he stared at her, Julia-Rae was fairly certain he like what he was seeing. Even though she only had on a white blouse and black dress pants. She hadn't counted on having a romantic encounter on this venture. "Well, I can assure you the only thing that will transpire tonight is me returning to my hotel room, slipping into a bathtub full of suds and then getting some sleep. My body aches from all that mountain climbing and I've a very early plane to catch tomorrow." Her words sounded harsh; Julia-Rae wondered why? Why was it that she wanted to stay on guard around him, what would be wrong about letting this handsome man get any closer to her? She remembered the musky smell of his aftershave and the hardness of his body as he pressed her against the stone wall. The heat of his hard chest, the press of his warm thighs. Damn, it had been a long time since she had been with a man. Hell who was she to kid, since her high schools days she'd only been to bed with one other guy besides Tim and he was Mr. In and Out, Shake It All About, then out like a light bulb. Neither experience had endured her to be excited at the prospect of lovemaking. So why was he so arousing?

"Hey, no need to get cranky. My mom always told me to wear clean dark underwear, keep my teeth brushed and never put sauerkraut on my hot dogs."

"What?"

"Leads to bad indigestion and worse it gives you ga…"

"I know what sauerkraut gives you, I meant why the dark underwear?"

"Hey accidents happen you know." He smiled, in such an innocent way and yet at the same time there was such an essence of mischievousness about him.

He must have been quite the devil as a boy. Julia-Rae found his humor infectious. It sure felt good to talk to someone besides business. In fact, talking to him seemed quite comfortable, almost like talking to herself. She hadn't expected this kind of conversation from a man dressed in tacky Peruvian smock, ragged blue jeans (albeit deliciously molded to his body like they had been shrunk to fit), and long blonde hair. Then again what did one expect to hear from the lips of someone with a tacky Peruvian smock? At least she was glad he'd chosen to dress in clean blue jeans and a bright blue cotton shirt. She'd thrown on suit pants and a plain white blouse she'd brought along for the return trip back.

"And are you ready to order now, sir." The waiter said as he returned.

"It's a good thing they serve western foods here also, I'm not in the mood for anything spicy. I'll go for the bratwurst, artichoke salad and lots of sauerkraut."

Julia-Rae looked up at him from the edge of her wineglass.

"Okay, so I was always a rebel, besides I've no intention of kissing anyone tonight either."

"Rest assured, after that meal you'll not get anyone within ten feet of you with anything flammable," she giggled. Yes, his humor was definitely infectious. Although she felt a bit insulted for not wanting her. That wasn't a page from her book of dating principals.

Roy let out a laugh that sounded as rich and as strong as the

Peruvian mountains. "Well, I didn't expect such humor from you.

You don't look the…"

"Didn't what?" The fire inside flared to ugly life, "look the type?"

"No," he replied, sounding apologetic. "Someone of your beauty and I suspect, passion, doesn't strike me as having a truly funny streak."

Those words hit a little hard. It had been true people often thought she didn't have much of a sense of humor. There were times she hated the color of her hair. She blushed, as he stared at her. “What I mean is that it’s quite nice to laugh with you, oddly heart warming.” He grew silent and as she sipped at her wine Julia-Rae also knew that those dark, sea blue eyes were studying her. His eyes, drinking in her beauty. He wanted her, that much was evident, no matter what he said, or how much sauerkraut he ate.

“Excuse me, I’ve got to go to the restroom.” Ray got up and abruptly walked away, a muffled buzz seemed to come from his pocket.

Julia-Rae thought she heard the muffled beep of a cellular phone just then. She rose as the waiter came by.

“Is everything okay?” He asked as she replaced her chair.

“Yes, just fine, I also need to visit the restroom, be right back.”

As Julia-Rae approached the door to the lady’s room she heard Roy’s muffled voice, talking to someone from just inside the door to the men’s room.

“Yes, everything’s great, we’re having dinner right now. Yes, together. I’ll explain what happened when I’m back, goodbye.”

Julia-Rae quickly entered the lady’s room. Curious to know what the phone call was all about. Oh well, it was probably none of her business anyway.

The rest of the meal went smoother, although Julia-Rae ended up drinking two more glasses of wine, true to his word he stuck to water.

Julia-Rae sank into the bubbles of her bath after, letting the silkiness of the bubbles wash over her she couldn’t help but smile. He had such an easy manner to himself and the amazing ability to make her laugh. She didn’t recall the last time she had so much fun with anyone, let alone a handsome man.

The wash of the bath bubbles felt like silken hands caressing her. Julia-Rae wished it was him. The image of

Roy here, naked, running his hands all over her body. She moaned and arched her back at the thought. Roy naked beside her. The very idea sent a shudder through Julia-Rae. Yes, she definitely wanted to meet him again and speaking of meeting it dawned on her she had forgotten to ask about the phone call. Oh, well it was probably none of her business anyways. She had noticed one thing though, that like her, he spent a lot of time in Edmonton. Julia-Rae did mention she was planning to go to a media event bungie jump. It was a promotional charity cause. Public figures were going to jump into a floating vat of Jell-O. He hadn't intended on being there, but Julia-Rae caught the look of want in his eyes as they parted. She knew he'd be there.

That was a sure bet.

Chapter Two

Julia-Rae stared at the stack of letters sitting on her desk. The majority, she knew would be bills. A sigh escaped her lips as she dropped her purse on the floor and plunked a handful of files on the only unused corner of the overloaded desk.

This was the part of running her own business that she didn't enjoy. Being the boss had its advantages, all right. It also had its headaches. Julia-Rae picked up the stack of unopened mail and put it with the files she had brought in. She would either deal with the mail later or have Cindy open it.

The ring of the phone startled Julia-Rae. "Hello, The Edge, the exciting magazine for today's woman, Julia-Rae speaking." She hoped it wasn't someone looking to collect on a bill. She wanted to get down to some serious work on her Machu Picchu piece, while it was still fresh in her mind.

“Hello dear, how’s the busy executive these days?” The familiar male voice on the other end of the phone asked. It was her dad, Dennis McNaughton.

“Oh good, I guess. I just got in. Dad, where are you phoning from?” She knew by the call display he was on his cell.

“I’m in town myself actually, on business and I thought we could do lunch.” The sound of his voice was reassuring. Her dad had always been there for her whenever she needed anything. In fact, it was his emotional and financial support that got her company off the planning stage and into a real life functioning business. Not to mention the fact that her dad had run his own company all his life and gave Julia-Rae much needed business information.

“Dad, I’d love to, say around 12:30 at Café Paridisio.”

“Sounds good on this end, see you there.”

Julia-Rae smiled. Her dad’s presence was always a welcome relief. Dennis had continuously encouraged his daughter to go after her dreams, even if they didn’t coincide with his plans for her. She knew that he probably wished he had a son instead of a daughter. She and Dennis did many things together, especially after her mother died. When she was a child, Dennis enlisted his daughter in all sorts of sports and other activities. Unfortunately, other than being a headstrong reckless tomboy, the only sport that really intrigued her was photography.

Julia-Rae loved capturing moments on film. Behind her on the wall hung an old black and white photo. The photo had been enlarged and computer enhanced. It was the only picture Julia-Rae had of her mom and why she wanted to capture rare moments on film. Her mom was dressed in a long fifties style skirt and ponytail and she sat on the back of a motorcycle. Carrie, her mother, looked free and rebellious, hair streaming back, bright red lipstick and a smile spread to each corner of her face. She looked for all the world like the carefree spirited woman that Julia-Rae was trying to instill as the appealing force of her magazine.

Her mother also strongly believed that a woman should stand up for what she wanted in life. It was a strong part of Julia-Rae's mother's character, she had been told by her grandmother and her dad. That's what set Julia-Rae's mind on starting up her own magazine, devoted to the adventuresome woman of today. The full-grown tomboy that lurked in a lot of ladies, once they got out of the office cast aside their prim and proper images and let their hair down. Women who threw on the tattered old jeans, sweatshirts and went off hiking in the backwoods or on some other adventure.

The driver, in the picture, was a young James Dean looking version of the voice that had just called, her dad. A moment in time captured on film that her mom had taken. Moments she had come to cherish as precious beyond belief.

The creak of the door into her office brought Julia-Rae out of her thoughts. “Good morning Julia-Rae, it’s good to have you back.” Spoke her secretary, Cindy Townsend. Cindy was much more then her secretary though. She was the right hand that virtually ran all of the day to day affairs in the office. Especially when Julia-Rae was out doing shoots for her next article. “The electric company had phoned to ask when they can expect their check and McBride’s phoned. They said the pictures for the last article haven’t turned out, something about being overexposed.”

“What?” Julia-Rae picked up the phone. “There had better be nothing wrong with those pictures. I sure can’t afford the expense of going back to Hong Kong to reshoot them.”

Cindy turned to leave. “Ah, Cindy, before I make this phone call can you look into the availability of a new zoom lens for my Nikon? I managed to have a gentleman break it for me and oh, I'll also need to know the cost to replace the lens. If possible, I'll need it for my next shoot. Are we still going to the West Edmonton Mall Media Bungie Event on Wednesday?"

"You bet and yes, I'll see what I can do about getting that lens ready for Wednesdays jump." Cindy nodded and left the room.

A smile came to Julia-Rae's lips. The lens reminded her of Roy Sutter. She'd been very tempted to invite him up to her room the other night. The thought of his delicious body, those hard arms holding her. A shiver of desire raced along her spine just as though she could imagine his tongue and his lips touching her, kissing her. Staring into those dark and timeless eyes, it was all she could do not to have him hold her hand at the dinner table.

He had given her his business card. Julia-Rae pulled it from her pocket and stared at it. Roy Sutter, Freelance

Photographer. She had called yesterday and left a message about the West Edmonton

Mall Media Bungie Jump. He'd be there, if the desire she saw in his eyes was real, she knew he'd be there. After the jump she planned on driving to Lake Louise the next day. She wanted to meet her old high school friend, Linda Barnes, another from the school of those expected to succeed in life. That was set up for the weekend, along with spending the day taking some pictures. Julia-Rae hadn't seen Linda in a long time and she'd never been out to Lake Louise in a very long time. Linda was working there, one of the managers of the Chateau Lake Louis. Her dad had taken Julia-Rae camping many times as a child in the mountains, never there. She wondered if the romantic atmosphere had anything to do with it. Romance was one thing her dad had cut out of his life after her mother died.

Romance; her thoughts drifted back to Roy. What was it about him that charmed her? Maybe his quirky sense of humor, humor too much like her own. Julia-Rae picked up the phone. The time for daydreaming was over, she had to attend to some serious business. This handsome man would have to take a backseat to work; that always came first.

"Hello, McBride's photography, Sammy speaking."

"Julia-Rae here, Sam, Cindy tells me that there's something wrong with the last batch of pictures I sent you?" She knew she should have developed that batch herself, like she usually does. But that would have meant waiting for them until she got back here.

"Oh, hi Julia-Rae, yes the first roll is overexposed, I can't use any of those pictures."

Damn, thought Julia-Rae, probably from going through the old metal detectors at the Hong Kong airport. The first roll had all of her good shots on it. "How about the second roll?"

"Yeah, I can save about twenty of those shots, but most of those pictures are only borderline shots."

“Okay, thanks, Sammy I’ll send Cindy over to get them and see what I’m going to do.” Julia-Rae hung up the phone in disgust. Now what? The article was already written for the next issue and the deadline was only a week away. She threw her hands over her face, the last time she did that the annoying lawyer had sauntered into her office. Suddenly the idea of having someone buy out her business seemed attractive.

“Yes, this is a serious offer to purchase your business.” Dennis McNaughton stared up at Julia-Rae from the documents she had unexpectedly dropped before him. In the background water glasses clinked and soft classical music played. It was an eclectic crowd at the Café Paridisio, a mixture from business suits to college kids, the kind of crowd that the café usually drew during the week. Dim lights accented original paintings hanging from the reclaimed brick walls. In Edmonton it was one of the few restaurants that possessed a chic California atmosphere.

"I guess I don't understand why, dad?" Julia-Rae was worried. She knew the Stanza group of magazines were her chief competition. They had a large glitzy corporate tower downtown with an office full of staff and they probably had the money to back up the offer.

"It's simple, your magazine is obviously making inroads into their market. They're hurting and that's why they are offering to buy you out. Congratulations, this is a sign that your magazine is doing well."

"But can they do anything, is what I want to know?"

"Well, you've got shares out there and if this company is serious then they'll be approaching the shareholders and start offering good dollar value to them, to entice them to sell. Usually a company interested in a merger or takeover will approach the biggest shareholders first, namely you."

"You mean they could buy me out?"

"Yes, theoretically, I'll have to go over the list of shareholders and see if any have been approached by this Stanza Corporation. This is the downfall of setting up a company with public shares."

Julia-Rae smiled back at her dad. His handsome, rugged features, although beginning to show signs of age, to be expected for a man of fifty-six, looked calm and at ease. The world of business was his home and only solace after Julia-Rae's mom died shortly after childbirth. He raised Julia-Rae virtually single-handedly. There were a few times her grandma looked after her, usually in the summer. Although Julia-Rae wished Dennis had spent some of his time getting another lady love in his life. Her dad never remarried. "So what can I do now, dad?"

"My suggestion would be to sell everything and come join my accounting business," he replied only half serious.

"Thanks dad, but I don't think so. Running this company, while it can be exhausting some days, is everything I've ever wanted to do. So thanks for the offer, but I'm very happy doing what I'm doing. Which is why I'm a bit upset by this proposal, I don't want anyone to yank the rug out from underneath me." The thought of working for his accounting company, sitting behind some computer desk and doing up financial statements had no appeal to Julia-Rae. She also knew that Dennis was thinking about retiring soon and really wanted her to be there to take over and run his company.

"Tell you what though, I'll do some digging for you, somehow that name rings a bell. Stanza? Can I hang on to these?"

"Sure." She knew her dad was hurt inside that she wasn't interested in being involved with his business. But she knew one of the things he admired, and promoted in his daughter, was her strength of character and her ability to stick to what she really wanted to do with her life.

"You are as strong-willed and stubborn as your mother."

Julia-Rae caught a brief misty look in his eyes. He got it sometimes even to this day when he talked about her mom. If he harbored any resentment to her mom's dying shortly after childbirth Dennis McNaughton never showed it to Julia-Rae. The man poured his heart into loving Julia-Rae. She felt just a little sorry for him, though. Dennis never remarried or barely dated after her mom died. "Dad can I ask you something about mom?"

"Sure."

"Why didn't you ever remarry?" Until now she never thought to ask her dad. Perhaps it was the incident with Roy that triggered her curiosity. Or maybe it was just time for her to hear what her dad had to say, in either case she wanted to hear the words from his lips. He sat there for a moment. “The truth?” “Yes, the truth.” His face was very sober.

“The truth is that I went out a few times on dates, but I couldn’t bring myself to erase the pain. I didn’t want to take the chance on being hurt again. So in the end I gave up and surrendered to the past. I threw all of my energy into pursuing my work and into raising you. I guess I fell into the trap of using my work as a crutch. A way of not getting involved again.”

His words stunned her. He had obviously done some deep thinking on this matter. “That’s true dad. I’ve seen you put all of your energy into your work, but you told me you’d never find another woman like her.” He’d always been very honest with Julia-Rae.

“The truth is Julia-Rae, I didn’t ever want to get hurt again. When Carrie died a big part of me died with her. It’s sad but in many respects, I know now I gave up living. Every morning I’d wake up and look over only to feel the cold sheet of her side of the bed and realize things weren't about to change. She was really gone.

Reality can be harsh sometimes. You know every date I went on I kept seeing your mother's qualities in the women or wishing they were more like her. Part of the truth was also, I knew there wasn't enough left inside of me to give to someone else. So, I focused on giving what love I had to running my business and to you. I don't want you to become like me and I'm afraid I've created that in you, Julia-Rae. You haven't allowed yourself to feel love, real love ever. I've watched you start this business and gave you the incentive to strive for what you wanted in life. To be able to stand by yourself. To not need anyone, like I still need your mother."

"But I don't want to feel the hurt you've gone through dad. I saw the anguish you suffered. As a child, I was maybe five or six and I remember coming downstairs once. I couldn't sleep, it was late and you were in the living room. I remember seeing a half empty bottle of whiskey and your wedding pictures beside you. You didn't see me standing there, but I do remember hearing you cry these deep wracking sobs. They were for mom I knew. Somewhere inside I knew that it wasn't safe to let myself get close to someone, anyone, if they were going to cause that much pain. I don't want to go through the pain you've gone through dad. I remember another time you were holding me in your arms and saying don't ever allow yourself to get hurt this bad. You made me promise you."

"Yes, I did that, but something I realized many years later was that in order to feel the hurt, the deep hurt over your mother's death, I had to experience the love first. I was wrong for demanding that of you. Sure, the loss was devastating, I cried for many years afterwards. But you know what? It took a long time to realize, I'd do it again in an instant if I could relive those moments we had together. Your mom and I had some incredible times together and those times make all that pain worthwhile. One doesn't know if their love will last forever or if it will be snatched away tomorrow. Please don't build that wall around your heart like I did, Julia-Rae.

Enjoy and treasure every precious moment. I've seen you throw all of your soul into this business and that's great, but please don't become what I have, a lonely man with no one to share my years with after I retire."

It was true, wasn't it, she thought. She was becoming a carbon copy of her dad. Julia-Rae thought of Roy and how rude she had been with him. Why would anyone want to go out with her after being treated like that? Not unless, her heart thumped hard, not unless he actually liked her.

"So while we're on that topic, I'm done spilling my guts and preaching to you. It's your turn," he said, "have you met any good men lately? I thought I saw a heard a tinge of excitement in your voice earlier."

He knew her all too well. Julia-Rae sat up a little higher. “As a matter of fact, I did, meet someone recently. It was on my last photo shoot. Dad, he’s got this crazy off the wall humor, he’s handsome and an absolute ass,” Julia-Rae smirked.

“He didn’t ask me out again, but I did mention I’d be at the Media Bungie Jump tomorrow. I’m pretty sure he’ll be there.”

“Well, he’s a damn fool to turn you down if he isn’t. I’d like to meet this fella someday if you and him click further and dear, don’t be so hard on him, give him a chance, go out on a few dates, enjoy yourself, you work too damn hard. There’s more to life I’m discovering then work. Did I tell you I’ve started playing golf?”

“No, you didn’t.” That was the first time her dad had ever mentioned any kind of pursuit other then work. Julia-Rae told him about how they met on her last photo shoot.

"Yeah I think I will call him. I had no real intentions of pursuing anything serious with him.

But perhaps a few dates to check him out would be a good idea."

Dennis glanced at his watch, "I've got to go."

As they were leaving the restaurant Dennis laughed out loud, "you didn't actually, ha, ha, ha, oh God! In the butt, you thwapped him with your bandanna in the butt, that's my girl. What a way to make an impression. I'm sure he'll not forget you." He shook his head as he opened the door to the awaiting cab. Dennis gave his daughter a big hug and a kiss on the forehead, before getting into the cab.

"Oh dad." It was something she always hated that he still did to her. But she knew that no matter what she did in her life, she'd always be his little girl. The one thing that kept Dennis McNaughton going all of these years, he told her many times. "Thanks dad, for the advice, business and personal, I really appreciate it."

“Ha, what’s an old fool good for other then telling his daughter how not to run her life. In the butt, what a crazy nut! He’s got to like you after that. Just as fiery as you always were, love ya my dear.” Dennis wiped aside a tear of gaiety and climbed into the waiting cab.

Julia-Rae watched him drive off. How could a man love a woman that much? That he’d want to spend his life alone. She couldn’t understand and yet the thought terrified her. She had seen her dad pining away his whole life just in the memory of Carrie. A woman she had never met and yet carried her blood and according to her dad, her temper. A love that strong, Julia-Rae shivered. Did she ever want to experience a love that strong? She was more like her dad then she realized. Only she hadn’t met the man worth pining over or worth the risk to let him get close to her. And that was a risk wasn’t it Julia-Rae, she told herself. Letting a man into her life and taking a chance on getting hurt.

Julia-Rae shook her head. Dennis always took her outbursts of temperamental fire with a large dose of humor. She couldn't ever recall a time when he got really mad at her for losing her cool. It was so unlike his demeanor and so. . ., so much like her mothers, she had been told. The one thing that she truly loved about her dad was that he accepted her as she was. Red hair and fireworks to boot.

As she walked back to her office she thought about working for her dad, the offer would always be there. Along with the chance to eventually run the entire company. Yet that seemed to be the easy road, she knew that while working for herself was less rewarding financially, at the moment, at least she was in control of her life. Knowing that somehow made up for the rest, or did it? A slight breeze sent a shiver through her. Roy's face came to mind and thoughts of the shivers she felt when he had her pinned up against that stonewall in Machu Picchu. She quietly walked the rest of the block to her office. "Okay then," she lifted her shoulders a little higher as she opened the door to her office. "Lets tackle those bill collectors head on, shall we?"

"Hot! She's a spicy one, that one," Antonio smiled. "She told you the fireworks that erupted when I told her I'd give her some time to look the documents over and I'd call back next week."

"Yes, I've already experienced that fire myself," Roy said as a little twinge of pain flared from his buttocks. This was a woman with the potential passion of a pent-up volcano brewing underneath. He definitely wanted to meet her again. "Is everything lined up for my trip to Lake Louise?"

Antonio smirked as he looked in his briefcase. He had worked with Roy for many years and handled all of his legal affairs. Including a few legal matters that dwelt close to the edge of being called shady. But even more, he had been a friend to this lone man who had very few friends in his life. Even a friend at times when no one wanted to call him a friend. Antonio had been there when Roy lost his wife in that terrible alcohol induced accident he had caused. He had also been there through the aftermath, when Roy had hovered on the edge of losing his life as he lay in a hospital bed. In fact Antonio engineered the publicity and legal haranguing afterwards to tune down the matter and keep the public out of what really happened. "Everything is here and in order. You'll have a room at the Chateau Lake Louise, overlooking the lake and I've confirmed with the hotel that she is indeed booked there also."

"Well, if she's there great, I think this will be one of my more pleasurable takeovers." A wistful smile broke Roy's lips. He ran one hand through his blonde hair. His fingers touched the ridge of the scar that lay there just above his left ear, a grim reminder of his past and the destruction he had wrought upon himself in his own life due to his over drinking. "Great, I think she'll be even more surprised to see me there at tomorrow's bungie jump event.

Antonio stared at his long-time friend. “Be careful on this one, they say he who rides the back of the tiger can often wind up inside.”

“Yeah, but this is one tiger I won’t mind getting a few claw marks from, if you know what I mean.” The very thought of having her deliciously naked beneath him sent a throb through Roy’s loins. What would it be like to hear her sigh his name as they made love? Roy shook his head, enough of the romantic notions. This was supposed to be a hostile takeover. Stick to the game plan, Roy.

Antonio turned to leave, “I’m serious, my friend, be a careful with this one she’s a tomcat.” He shook his hand as if his fingers were on fire.

“Thanks for the concern, but I can handle myself just fine.” Roy looked at his airline ticket as Antonio stepped out of his office. He knew Antonio was gravely concerned. Which was most unlike the native Italian, he usually had a cool reserve to himself. Did Antonio sense something Roy didn't?

Roy knew that Antonio had lost a lot of face when Julia-Rae threw him out of her office and that was something Roy knew that Antonio feared above anything else. He knew Antonio wouldn't rest now until the takeover of her company was done. Roy thought back to the scene at Machu Picchu. The softness, the hunger in her eyes and the heat of her sweet body as he pressed her up against the wall. He didn't miss the anger in her eyes, the hurt and the passion. She had tried to hide it, but Roy caught that too. The deep driving passionate furies that resided in Julia-Rae McNaughton. Furies he couldn't wait to unleash.

Julia-Rae stared up and looked at the structure nearly two hundred feet above her. A small gathering of local celebrities, politicians and media milled about. They were all here to celebrate the opening of the Bungie Zone jump. Many had come to cheer everyone else on, there didn't look like many would do the actual deed of jumping.

"Well, are you ready girl?" Cindy asked.

Cindy had come along for moral support and to take a few pictures of the event. Pictures to be used, perhaps for an upcoming article of the magazine.

"As ready as I'll ever get." The idea of jumping sent a pale of white through Julia-Rae. She hadn't realized just how high two hundred feet really was until this moment.

"Then that makes two of us," spoke a deep male voice.

Julia-Rae turned around and was astonished to see Roy standing there. Only this time he was dressed far better than the clothes he had on him last time. The man had come outfitted in bowtie, white ruffled shirt and black tuxedo, complete with tails. The sight managed to take the words from her throat for a moment. "Ah, what's with the outfit?" was all she managed to get past her lips.

"Well if you gotta go, you gotta go in style." He smiled. "Besides I thought it would great in the promo pictures."

"Well, you'll definitely attract attention in that outfit. Although it looks more like you're dressed for an evening gala dinner or a. . ." The words stuck in her throat.

"A wedding," he said softly as he took her hand and kissed it. "It's good to see you again."

Her heart thudded to a stop as electricity raced along her arm at his touch and his soft kiss. She had wanted to say wedding, also, but the thought had sent images of him standing at the alter holding her in his arms. Chills sank into the pit of her stomach. This man was too much for her senses to take.

"A-hem." Broke the silence.

"Ah yes." She pulled her arm back as if struck by a hot errant ash from a fire. "Let me introduce my associate and right hand, Cindy Townsend."

"Roy Sutter, glad to meet your acquaintance." He merely shook her hand.

Julia-Rae could tell she was hoping to get a kiss on her hand also.

"Now that we're introduced let me see when we get to do the jump. Care for a glass of wine, for yourself, might settle your nerves."

"Do I look a little nervous?"

"White, you look marvelous in petrified white, is the color I'd call your face."

"I guess, I am. Yes, a glass would be nice." Minutes later they were ready to jump.

"Okay lets do it." Julia-Rae said again as she slowly began to climb up the spiral staircase, to the awaiting platform of the bungie jump just above her. The entire setup was mounted inside the West Edmonton Mall Waterpark, suspended from the roof on great steel wires. Every step Julia-Rae took started a slow unsettling sway from the structure. Her knuckles whitened every time she grabbed the railing, reluctant to let go of its security. Below her, nearly two hundred feet down, floating on the waters of the gigantic pool of the water park, was a huge vat of red wiggly Jell-o. "God, why couldn't they have picked another color other then red."

Roy, who was climbing up right behind her, replied. "What? Just because it looks like blood, does that scare you? Besides if something goes wrong there's less of a mess to clean up." He had a hard time not taking his mind off the figure before him. Julia-Rae had worn an older pair of rather snug fitting jeans and she looked rather delectable.

"You are sick, did your mother ever tell you that?"

"Only when she unlocked my chains and let me out of my room."

Julia-Rae shook her head, she enjoyed his usual witty and humorous replies. What she would have enjoyed more right now though, was having the entire structure she was climbing stay still. Very still. Maybe this wasn't such a great idea after all. "The things I do for publicity." The whole stunt, having media jump into a vat of Jello, was set up to raise funds for disabled kids, in addition to promoting the West Edmonton Waterpark and the opening of the new Bungie Ride. All Julia-Rae knew for sure was this was going to scare the hell out of her, get her sticky and gooey and allow her to spend some time with Roy. She only hoped it was worth it.

"Say - did you get your will up to date?"

"Knock it off Roy."

"Just checking, just checking. What happened to that crazy devil may care attitude you had back up the mountain?"

"Left it besides my nerves, yesterdays dinner and the glass of wine I just had if we don't get this over with quick."

Roy definitely had a flair for style though. She couldn't get out of her mind what it would be like to be standing beside him dressed in the long flowing white gown of a wedding dress. That thought sent even more shivers through her then the idea of jumping over a platform into a vat of Jell-o with only an overgrown elastic band tied around her ankles.

As she reached the top there was a cameraman there, from a local news station, along with Cindy. Both were taking pictures of the event. Actually the image of him dressed up in a wedding style tuxedo would look great in some of the shots Cindy was taking for her magazine.

"Ms. McNaughton?" Asked the young attendant, too young to really look like he knew what he was doing.

"Ah, yes." Her stomach was slowly becoming a mass of fluttering butterflies as she looked over the edge and stared at the now rather small looking vat of Jell-o.

"First rule up here is don't look down," the attendant said bluntly.

"You shouldn't have said that." Roy snapped and grabbed Julia-Rae's chin. "My bloodshot eyes, stare into them, remember?" The hurtling train down the mountainside and him hold her. That she wouldn't forget. "Have you ever done this before Roy? You look rather calm."

"Actually yes, in the jungles of Borneo some of the tribes use a form of bungie jumping as a way of a boy entering manhood. Only they use vines tied around the feet and they jump from tall trees."

"Into water?"

"No, over land. Every once in awhile the vines break and the boys crack their heads open, they probably have an 80% success rate."

"Oh, and you tried this?"

"Yes. Only men are allowed into the tribe's talking circles. No outsiders that had not taken the initiation, would be allowed to take pictures or intermingle with the tribe."

"Oh, you've been around, haven't you?"

"It's okay Ms. McNaughton. In order for us to get insurance we have to ensure a 99% success rate otherwise we lose our bond," answered the attendant as he was taking measurements of Julia-Rae's body.

"Oh, how comforting to know." She replied, suddenly very worried of that one percent. "Is that a better safety record than flying?" She hated flying, well the flying part isn't what she hated. She hated the part where the tail fin breaks off and suddenly you are not flying. This man had traveled to places she had only dreamed of and did things she wouldn't have the guts to perform. "Okay let's get this over with."

"About the same factor, although I think plane's are safer. Your weight is?"

"About one ten, why?"

"I have to know in order to get the right cord for your jump."

"If I'm wrong?"

"Too much weight is no big deal, but not enough weight compensation and you'll slice through the Jell-o holding tank into the water and crack your head open on the bottom of the pool."

"Oh." Suddenly the hearty meal at lunch didn't seem like a good idea. It might add an extra pound or two, she thought. "Okay, are you two jumping separately or together?"

"Sep. . ."

Roy stepped closer to her, until the she could feel the heat of his body. "Together," he said loudly. "I'm one ninety-five."

"Done."

Julia-Rae hadn't anticipated this. She was speechless as ropes were thrown over them, before she had a chance to protest. Thick cords were tied to their ankles. They were now bound together. Roy's arms went around her. Julia-Rae stared into his eyes, his breath hot against her neck. The butterflies fluttering in her stomach were zapped by a wave of electricity. The surge of having him holding her, touching her in his strong arms was reassuring and comforting. She hadn't even thought what he would feel like pressed up against her. The sensual smell of his cologne, his eyes staring at her like she had no clothes on and they were pressed naked together. His stare so much like the hungry look of a prowling lion and she was caught in that passionate, vision. Cunning, hot and deadly. A silent moan escaped her lips as she felt the ripple in his arms tightening around her.

"Okay, slowly slide over to the edge." The attendant said.

She hadn't even realized that they were now bound together at the feet and at the waist. His intoxicating presence stripped all sense of reason, of anything beyond the circle of his arms she wanted to melt into. All that really registered was the hard press of his body, the comfort of his arms and the hunger of her soul.

"Okay, on the count of five, then."

She had only five seconds to enjoy this moment.

"Four."

Why couldn't it be like this forever?

"Three."

She trembled. Roy's arms closed tighter about her.

"Two."

Automatically Julia-Rae reached around with both arms to pull Roy closer to her. She looked into his eyes. The distance between their lips decreased as he bent his head to hers.

"One."

Involuntarily she parted her lips, wanting his lips against her, kissing her, releasing her from the hunger that had began to build inside of her and him, she could feel him stirring against her. The hunger of wanting him, from the first moment she laid eyes on him.

Roy flexed his body and flung the two of them from the edge of the platform. Another second and his lips would have been kissing hers. It was all he could do to stop from kissing her. She felt so soft, so nearly helpless in his arms, so tiny. He had instinctively pulled her into him. He wanted nothing more then to hold her, protect her and, he stopped for a moment, make love to her. The thought hit hard.

Both stared and screamed as the blob of Jell-o increased rapidly in size. Julia-Rae felt her stomach make its way up her throat, clawing to get out as they hurtled down with ever increasing speed.

The red Jell-o grew until it filled Julia-Rae's entire spectrum of vision. She closed her eyes as they smacked into the wiggly mass of Jell-o. Before Julia-Rae could realize it the Jell-o was gone and she was being effortlessly sucked upwards. Looking over her shoulder the platform they jumped from grew again in size until it seemed too frighteningly near. Close enough she swore she could reach out and touch it.

The flash of camera lights, like an explosion of fireworks, jarred her attention back to Roy, to his arms. For a fraction of a second they hung suspended in space, wrapped in each others arms reaching the apex of this rebound. In that brief moment as she stared into his eyes, Julia-Rae knew she was beginning to lose something. She liked being held in his arms, surrounded by his protective energy. Desired it, she pulled tighter into him.

Then gravity reclaimed its rights to their bodies. Down they hurtled again, only this time they never entered the pool of Jell-o.

"All right," Roy and Julia-Rae hollered in unison as they bounced up and down a few more times. A rowboat began to approach them from the edge of the pool as they swayed helplessly about thirty feet above the waters of the park.

Roy stuck his tongue out and licked at a blob of Jell-o stuck on her cheek. "Hmm, delicious. Definitely delicious."

"Oh." Julia-Rae gasped at his audacity and shivered in response as a new set of emotions, not stirred by the act of being scared senseless, peeled themselves across her traumatized nerves.

Finally, they were lowered into a rowboat that was waiting below them. As Julia-Rae entered the safety of the rowboat Julia-Rae found herself unable to speak. Her entire body couldn't stop shaking from the adrenalin charging through her, either from the ride or being pressed up against him, or both?

"Wow, wasn't that a blast." Roy let out a holler.

She smiled, trembling.

"You okay, you look like you're going to be sick or something?"

"It's just the excitement and my lunch don't seem to be getting along." Julia-Rae lied. It was far more than that. "I need to get out of this boat and grab something at home to settle my stomach."

"Can I give you a ride?"

"No, I'll be okay." Would she ever be okay after today? The rest of the event was a blur as the electricity racing through her body rifled of all sanity, before it settled down. As she drove home the exhilaration of the night still raced through her spine. But it was not the thrill of the ride or the terror of being flung headlong over a two hundred foot precipice.

No, the elation of being in his arms again, staring into his eyes, the very erotic act of him licking her cheek, wishing he could be licking other places. Knowing that for the first time in her life, she was no longer alone. There was someone else that needed, who had to be there, to make her feel complete. Was this what drove her dad to be alone all those years, this feeling, this desire, this need? The need to have someone else there, to share her life with. To let get close to her.

Julia-Rae got out of her car and nearly ran to the door of her condo. She slammed the door and stood just inside the door, letting the walls of her personal world of safety hold her up, in a world that was no longer safe and secure. No longer could she shut out everyone. No longer did she not need anyone, instead hunger tore at her needs. Tears streamed down her face. "No one said this was going to be easy girl."

Chapter Three

Roy sipped at the Earl Gray tea. Mrs. Leighton sat staring out at the wind whipping through the trees. Her rocking chair creaked as she moved in it.

"Yes, my old bones are telling me winter's coming early this year." Her voice was shaky belaying her years. Roy watched her adjust the shawl that she habitually wore. She took another sip of tea, brittle hands shaking as she raised the teacup to her lips. Roy knew Mrs. Leighton hadn't too many years left on this earth, she was eighty-four. He smiled at her. Since her husband and only daughter, Carrie, had died she had been merely biding time. Biding time in a place that beat an old worn out message with no meaning left for her.

Roy stared out the window of the old townhouse. A row of townhouses, exactly like hers stared back. This area of town, the south side of Edmonton just north of Whyte

Avenue while once stately, was now a little rundown and showing its age. Large graceful trees lined the boulevard. The trees waved in the wind, a few leaves shook loose. It was early September and already the trees were starting the colorful procession into winter. Winter came early enough every year to Edmonton and seemed to hang around a couple of months too long. Fall was the time of the year Roy enjoyed. The varied colors of the leaves and the morning frost made for spectacular pictures. He couldn't wait to get to the Rockies on Friday, partly to meet Julia-Rae and partly to take some fall pictures in the mountains. He turned, returning to his present company. "How's the tea?"

"A bit brisk, but it soothes the old bones."

"I can water it down a little."

"No, I'll be okay. Say did you bring me a new romance novel?"

"Yes, as a matter of fact I did. This one is called 'Colorado Weekend'. It's about a hotel owner and a client who stays for the weekend. Each is immediately attracted to the other."

"I hope this one is a little steamier than the last one," Mrs. Leighton frowned.

"Yes, I got the hint after trying to read you that last historical. Don't worry this is one of those red hot cover books that you like.

But you know I hate getting you all, ah- "

"Hot and bothered, is that what you wanted to say."

"Yes," Roy smiled. He didn't want to offend her.

"Hey, at my age, you get what you can get, and you reading me steamy romances is about as close to sex as I'll get." She laughed and began coughing until Roy was afraid a lung would pop out of her mouth.

"Mrs. Leighton!" Roy was mortified that she would say such a thing at her age. Getting her excited was something he didn't want to do. "I can see the headlines now:

Elderly Woman Found Dead Of Heart Attack, Man Caught and Arrested for Reading Her Explicit Romance Stories."

"Huh, just because I'm older, that doesn't mean that I was an angel in my younger days. Although I think the last time I made love was probably before you were born." She snorted and coughed up the other lung. "Oh dear, besides how many woman at my age can say they got a handsome hunk of a man whispering dirty nasties from a romance novel in their ear."

"Mrs. Leighton!" Roy opened the book to hide his embarrassment and the smile that threatened to spill over into laughter. For an old gal she sure had character, he had to admit. But then he always enjoyed people with character, especially women. "Okay, ready to go?"

"Just a minute, darn near lost my teeth." She snapped her teeth back into place. "Okay, I'm ready." She settled back in the rocking chair, hands on her lap and closed her eyes. She popped one eye open. "Oh and don't be glossing over any of the good stuff or Mr. Earl Gray here will be decorating that snazzy pullover of yours." She pointed to her tea cup.

Roy shook his head, what a lady. He had known her for the last fifteen years. While Mrs. Leighton had really gone downhill, health wise, in the last couple years, since her husband died, she still carried that fire and spunk that he admired. Spunk, he knew, she'd carry to her grave. He could picture her in her coffin. Everyone wailing away and her suddenly lifting her head up, saying something like, "Can the crying already, you're going to get the rugs soaked with those tears, now someone run along and get me a blanket, its damn cold in this pine box." He laughed to himself. Maybe that was why he still came over and visited her every couple of weeks. Or maybe it was the one last thing that he couldn't let go from his past. His way of somehow repaying the guilt and the debt for what he had done.

"Hey, ya going to read that thing or wait for the pages to rot out?" Roy shook his head and began to read.

Colorado Weekend by Felicity Talaisman

Mickey's left hand at ten, his right at two filled the vision of the Astoria hotel's front desk clerk.

Connie Moore rounded the corner from her office and saw Samuel, the desk clerk, arguing with a virtually naked man. The man bore only a bath towel, at least a size too small, tucked precariously around his midsection. A trail of wet, soapy footprints, mixed with wiggling pools of iridescent soap bubbles, led from the ornate hotel elevator across the rich, deep green mint colored, Berber carpeted lobby.

Walking up from behind, Connie took note of the man's dimensions, something grilled into her from her years of being on the police academy: white Caucasian, around six two, slightly tanned, light brown hair, bearing what looked like a Mickey Mouse watch on his wrist and judging by the massive vee and ripples of muscles on his back, extremely well built and probably not too intelligent after all who'd wear a watch into a bath. Snap judgment, aggressive, possible weight lifter strung out on steroids.

Use caution, her hand instinctively reached for the holster to the gun she no longer wore.

Connie glanced around the lobby set in a Rococo theme, with its pastel shaded panels carved with cherubs cavorting in garland. Fortunately, there were no other patrons milling about at this time of the afternoon.

"I asked for the hotel manager," he demanded in a deep and powerful voice.

Connie walked around to where Samuel was sadly dangling on the end of this gorillas arm. Everything about this man spoke of strength and male virility. From the ripple in the flex of his ample biceps, to the ridges standing out underneath the mat of chest hair that descended in a dark vee down the center of his chest. It seemed to be no effort, to the man, to be hoisting Samuel off the ground. He reminded her of that rare testosterone poisoned version of a male that rarely existed these days. Everything from the hard solid contours of his rear and oak thick cords of his thighs to the square cut deep cleft jaw. He didn't belong here in this age. He belonged to some barbaric age, a warrior of bygone times, quick, powerful and deadly. A man that lived and survived by the honed sharpness of his wits.

As he turned to confront Connie, she caught the small jagged scar just behind his left ear.

"What seems to . . ."

"He ack…" Samuel tried to respond but was unable with his shirt collar scrunched around his neck and the man's fist.

She had handled bigger, before. Connie stood her ground as he stared hard at her. Many a man had unsuccessfully tried to browbeat her down. She knew from her training that the initial contact in confrontational situations was crucial. For another moment neither gave any quarter; finally he glared down at her tag. She breathed a little easier. The situation, though tense, was manageable. She had established her ground.

"I said I asked for the . . ."

"And I sir, am the hotel manager, and before I discuss anything with you, you will let go of my desk clerk." She caught the nearly imperceptible rise of his eyebrows.

Caught off-guard Clay Holden, did as he was told and lowered Samuel to the ground. He hadn't expected a skirt to come here, let alone be the manager. "Ah, sorry, didn't expect a skirt." He also hadn't expected her to be a gorgeous brunette. She wore a typical corporate style uniform, with a dress ending just below the knee. The kind of uniform meant to fit all shapes and sizes, but normally only looked good hanging on a rack. The suit did nothing to hide her curves. The brunette looked so assertive standing there with her hands planted on her hips and chestnut colored hair cast in a fiery hue by the hotel's lighting. Something very sexy in that.

She didn't seem fazed or intimidated either, that struck a chord of respect in his heart and an excited throb to another part of his anatomy. She hadn't backed away when he challenged her with his initial stare. Her face flushed a subtle red and her lips held a full, sultry quality to them. Lips meant to be kissed; fiercely and hotly. Yet, her eyes bore a look of well-worn harshness, too familiar on such a beautiful face. He had learned long ago to read peoples faces in his career; it saved his life many times as a detective.

The manager stood her ground well, if she was afraid of him or felt intimidated, he hadn't caught it in her eyes. But in those eyes of soft, tropical island water blue he saw himself reflected and Clay knew she could lead him anywhere. Eyes he could have been staring into while camped out on the grassy mountainside of Mt. Kilimanjaro. While across the hot languid savanna, lions roared as they lay with each other, bellowing a hungry lust and at night, the distant thunder of tribal drums pounded a compelling, sensual beat. Or instead, on a mist-coated car of the Orient Express train, bound for some exotic city, name unpronounceable, as it glided through the night. Dim lights overhead flickering in rhythm to the maddened click of the railway ties below. In rhythm to each maddened click of his heart.

Clay shook his head. Damn he shouldn't have read that gritty romantic adventure novel on the train ride here. Yet, something about this woman that he knew nothing about, raised hot temp of his heart.

"Clay Holden and you have my apology, I've been overstressed at work recently and had decided to take a holiday here," he said as he extended his hand over the counter. It was partly the truth, he had elected to take this assignment, to get a bit of break from dealing with the hard-core people on the streets of LA. A place where you always had to watch your back and no man was a friend.

She seemed to hesitate for a moment before she extended her hand in greeting. The touch sent an erotic jolt through him. He wanted to yank her across the desk and pull her to him, crushing those red lips to his. Clay thought better of it. It wasn't appropriate, this time.

"Apology accepted. Connie Moore, Manager of the Astoria Hotel." Connie watched his anger recede like a tide that beats relentless against the beach. Until all that remained was a calm. A calm born of an easy strength, she liked to think of it as a masculine grace. A grace some men carried so naturally well. That easy flowing strength born of being in control, living beyond the boundary of fear. Like the male lion that saunters through the jungle. It was a feature some men possessed that Connie found very attractive.

In the wake of his anger, mirrored in those eyes of the darkest brown, she saw places she'd long forgotten about.

Hot, summer nights. Sweating dripping from her naked body and from his. Cries of passion and hungers deep pleasures. Connie had hesitated before touching his hand. She knew what this incredible specimen of a male wanted to do with her. Perhaps if they were alone he would do what his eyes spoke. Would she resist? Memories of Alan grabbing her from behind, like he used to do and sliding his naked body next to hers. His hands virtually tearing away her clothes, stripping all civility from her and possessing her, pleasuring himself and her. Connie had tried to forget about memories like that, they were too brutally arousing to deal with on cold, lonely nights. Nights when the queen-sized bed seemed like an unending desert and her stranded somewhere under a hot blazing sun, hopelessly alone.

Would Clay pull her across this front counter and ravish her body with his hard lips? Run his hands over her and pull her protective clothing from her? Connie shuddered. He reminded her too much of Alan, her deceased fiancée, shot dead while on duty one night. It had been six long years of being alone, of shutting down any sensual emotions, of denying herself the pleasures she once loved to experience. His hand, rough, hard, just one touch had awoken all of that. As they released hands he ran his fingertips along her palm. Electric shivers shuddered their way across her. A stab of want ached at her center. Hunger, for him, God she hadn't been like this for a long time. Somewhere in the back of her most intimate thoughts, she knew he had already taken control. The bastard.

Every nerve cried to run and lock herself in the safety of her office. "How can I help you, Clay Holden?"

"Two things. One, I was taking a quote 'luxurious bubble bath' as stated in your hotel's brochure and after using over half the bottle found out that there aren't even enough suds to coat the tub. Two, I had stepped out to grab some ice and realized I had locked myself out of my room. This employee of yours informs me, as I'm standing here cold, wet and naked, that I am not registered in this hotel and that without proper ID he cannot allow me into the room."

Samuel straightened his tie. "Sir, the hotels policy is quite clear on allowing anyone the use of an extra key, especially when not registered with the hotel."

"Ah Samuel just hang on, Mr. Holden here, obviously has come from somewhere in this hotel, it's too cold outside to be walking around naked. Now what room did you say you are in?"

"212."

Connie checked the register, but sure enough his name wasn't there. "Okay Mr. Holden there's obviously been a mix-up. I will shall get a spare key and escort you to room 212, where I presume you have some ID."

"Yes, and what about the bubble bath?"

"Well, I can assure you that if the hotels brochure states we provide luxurious bubble baths, we will provide you with a luxurious bubble bath and I will make sure this matter is handled, personally." She reached for a business card out of habit and stopped when she realized he had no place to put it.

"Good, then I can expect to see you up in my room, right away?"

"I'll escort you personally with a key."

He had said that more as a command than a question. Had she just said personally? Alone in his room. She had caught the slight sneer on his face, yes, he'd definitely try something.

Clay stepped backwards. A cool rush of air reminded him that he bore no clothes and only a precariously tucked, undersized bath towel. Even more precariously tucked since his awakening desire had begun to push at the confines of the towel. Clay's cheeks heated up. Touching Connie had awakened more then just mental want.

Clay strode as dignified from the lobby as possible, the ludicrousness of his situation just dawned on him. He could read the local headlines now, "With his manhood singing O'Canada, undercover detective found prowling in local hotel lobby naked." So much for being discreet with this assignment.

Still as an older couple entered the lobby, at least he was certain she hadn't seen his arousal.

One thing he knew, before this weekend was out, not only would he get what he came here for but he'd get to know more then Connie's name. It wasn't often a woman elicited such a response from him, Clayton Holden, LA detective. "Perhaps one hell of a long, cold shower is more in order." He muttered to himself as he entered the elevator.

Connie came in behind him.

Roy closed the book. "I'll finish this next week. I gotta take off for an airplane flight." He sipped at the cooling tea. The intense feelings the main character in the book, Clay Holden, was feeling for the heroine, Connie, he could relate to. It was too similar to the intensity he was starting to feel for Julia-Rae. Maybe Antonio was right, maybe he had better be careful around her.

Mrs. Leighton slowly reached for her tea, “Whew, sounds like it’s going to be one of those scorchers the devil reads around the dinner table just to torture the poor souls in hell. Although, I’m having a bit of a struggle with the romantic thoughts the hero is having. The men I’ve met around here certainly don’t talk that way. But ya know it’s only a book. Here I’ve signed that last book for you; you can keep it for a memento.”

Roy thought about her words as he opened the cover to the romance book. She had written, To Ray Thanks for all of those hot passionate nights spent in enjoyment with you, this book and the nights to come. Love Angie. “You’re incorrigible Mrs. Leighton, you really are, thank you.” Every book he had ever read her she had signed and left a thank you note written inside. Usually written with some sort of highly suggestive notes. He sometimes read the romance novels before going to bed. It was intriguing how women thought and how much they enjoyed the courtship and all the other events leading up to the accumulation of the relationship. It was funny Roy thought that was one of the basic differences between men and women. Most men usually enjoyed everything after the real sex part started. In any case the novels got him to better understand what women are looking for when he was on a photographic assignment.

Mrs. Leighton truly was quite a character. “Well, you know I’ve been keeping a journal. It’s something my therapist convinced me to do since the accident.” Roy said and added. “When I go back and reread some of my thoughts, they are romantic and passionate. I surprise myself; I never took myself for the die-hard, romantic type.”

“This coming from the man who comes over and reads romance books to little old ladies and takes pictures that should be framing the covers of those books. You better take a closer look at what really is inside that sexy body of yours." She looked up at Roy as he sat there, sipping the tea and quietly staring at her pictures on the mantel. She knew which picture he was staring at. "You know Roy, it's been a long time since Carrie died."

"I know." He hung his head a little. Lessons in life come pretty hard sometimes and Roy still blamed himself for this one. Keeping a journal going after all was part of his therapy. It helped to erase most of the pain and sorrow for what had happened. Still there were moments when the anguish overwhelmed him and he wished it could have been him and not Carrie that died that night. Still, the journal seemed like an old friend at times, nearly the oldest one he had.

"You really should think about getting a lady in your life. Eight years is enough time for mourning. You need to get on with living again."

"I know," he repeated. He fought to hold back a tear. "But since Carrie died a part of me died also." Roy stared up at his old wedding picture on the mantel.

Mrs. Leighton shook her head. "So a part of you died. That's okay, but life is about living you know. And when you're alive you grow and rebuild that part that's gone. Rebuild and relearn."

Her words rang hollowly through Roy's ears as he rose and put away the silver platter. Part of him was thinking that for being an old bird she sure had some wise things to say. So why did he feel such strong guilt for how he was feeling around Julia-Rae? Feeling for her? Damn, he was just supposed to be seducing her. "Catch you later, Mrs. Leighton." He said as he closed the door to the condo. Business, this was strictly business.

The knock on her hotel room door startled Julia-Rae. She had just booked into the Chateau Lake Louise and was in the middle of unpacking her suitcase. “Yes?”

“Let me in so I can give you a big hug, girlfriend.”

“Iiiii-e Linda!” she screamed overcome with delight. “I missed my old sorority roommate at the check in.” Julia-Rae yanked open the door and was rewarded by the sight of her blonde-haired friend flinging herself into her arms. The two screamed and cried, for a moment, like seven-year-old girls. “Oh god, it’s been too long. Let me have a good look at you girl.” Julia-Rae grabbed Linda’s hand, led her to the full-length mirror and stepped back in admiration.

“God, you’re looking good lady. It has been what, two years?” Linda was dressed in her corporate CP hotel staff uniform.

“Look at you girl, you’ve still got that slender figure.”

“And look at you girl, you’ve still got all those curves.”

"Do you remember when we'd go out to those dance clubs? Man, we'd turn men's heads." Julia-Rae asked.

"Yeah, I was just thinking that same thing. We were quite the pair."

"I swear men would drool over us. I've got time for a quick bite before going back to work, care to join me for coffee and a snack down in the staff lunch room?" Linda said.

"Sure." The two walked from her room and headed for the ornate elevator. "Speaking of men, have you got any lucky guys in your life?" It had been a long time since Julia-Rae had even talked to Linda.

"Well up to this weekend, I was going to say not really, except I met this gorgeous hunk of a rancher last weekend. I think he owns a ranch near Olds Alberta and he's coming back here this weekend.

Can't get enough of me I think."

"You always went for those brawny, take them by the horns type of guys."

"There's something to be said about the scent of a sweaty hard working man. Especially with the aroma of leather on them, especially in the bedroom. And you, still swearing off men?"

Julia-Rae knew Linda liked some forms of S&M in the bedroom, not her thing, and that she was referring to the incident back in their university days, Tim had nearly raped her. Linda held her in her arms most of the night as Julia-Rae cried her eyes out. Julia-Rae also had to restrain Linda from wanting to cut off his excuse for wearing jockey shorts.

They entered the elevator and went back to the main floor. Linda led her through the main dining room to a small area just inside the kitchen where there were a dozen plain tables were set up. "Hope you don't mind the Spartan surroundings, this is where the staff eat."

"No, actually I met this hunk of a man, while on a photography assignment at Machu Picchu. He's got blonde dirty hair, that should be cut to look a little more respectable and like me he's also does

freelance photog and his name is Roy Sutter."

Linda's mouth fell open. "Oh my God, he's here."

"What do you mean, here?"

"I went over the guest list and register like I always do, looking to make sure your name was on it and I remember that name on the list."

"Are you sure?"

"Yes, I'm sure, that's one of my jobs to know who's here, the times they'll be eating and if they have any special requirements. He's booked in room 442 under a corporate rate, in fact it was a last minute booking, cost a bundle to get him in, I remember the front desk asking if they could squeeze one more in for dinner. Were you expecting him?"

"Yes. I mean no. I mean, oh I don't know what I mean. I did mention to him I'd be busy here this weekend." Julia-Rae quickly explained the events of the past week and a half. Especially about being tied together at West Edmonton Mall's Waterpark.

"Well honey, I don't think he's got picture taking on his mind this weekend."

"What am I going to do if he asks me out for supper, I haven't got a thing to wear."

"Hey, remember all the times we swapped clothes in university? You can come up later when I get off work, we can crack open a bottle of wine talk about old times. I've got some looser fitting dresses that may fit you. I think I can compress you into one of them."

"Men."

"Yeah, talk about men and try on clothes."

"I'd love to, thanks Linda."

“I’m glad for you Julia-Rae. I was so worried about you after that last episode with Tim. I was sure you were going to swear off men forever and turn gay or something. I know you’re not much of the actively chasing type, but you sure shut half the human race right out of your life.”

“Yes, I know. I had this same discussion with my dad over lunch just the over day. I guess like you my focus became my studies and then my work. I wanted to become successful in my life and I didn’t need a man to do that.”

“And now you’ve attracted the right one for you. I read somewhere that when the time is right and you’ve not put energy into pursuing members of the opposite sex or have energy tied into previous relationships you will attract the man you seek. The one that is most compatible to your needs, most aligned with your energy and chakras.”

“Oh, you were always into that woo-woo stuff, weren’t you. Yeah, but I wasn’t seeking anyone.”

"Well, he's here, nothing in life is a coincidence I've read. Everything happens to us for a reason Julia-Rae. Besides you told him you'd be here, right."

Julia-Rae thought about that for a moment. Perhaps there was a lot of truth there. She remembered meeting Linda at a time in her life when she had never had a truly close girlfriend, someone that she could share everything with, even stories about their lovers. And there was Linda in her dorm room, her roommate, on the first day of classes. After all of these years Linda was still her tightest and best friend. Julia-Rae had asked the universe for her and got it. Perhaps Linda had a good point about attracting Roy and herself, into Julia-Rae's life. Julia-Rae thought it was some kind of fluke that Linda had showed up in her life.

Linda also had a spiritual dimension to her that Julia-Rae never seemed to possess. It was a fresh perspective on life and Julia-Rae welcomed it into her heart. "So here we are two career girls, successful and still as crazy as ever." They both smiled, laughed and hugged each other.

"Life just doesn't get any better then this does it? Wine it is, see you after I get off at eight." Linda gave Julia-Rae a big hug and sauntered off. She sat there wondering if this man was for real. He booked a last minute reservation in order to get here, or just take the chance that this was the hotel she was booked at? Her heart hammered away at the realization that this man was here for her and only her. Would he like her still? Could she trust herself to let him get close? Oh please girl, trust that this one isn't going to hurt you like the last one, she thought.

Chapter Four

The sheer rock wall of Mt. Fairview on her left and the gentler pine tree laden slopes of Beehive to her right greeted Julia-Rae as she stood on the front patio of the Chateau Lake Louise Hotel. At the far end of the valley where it came to a vee rested majestic, snow-capped Mt. Victoria. The glacier that lay snuggling on Mt. Victoria's slopes held the birth-waters of Lake Louise. The picturesque, silty, emerald-blue hues of Lake Louise, lay between these three mountains, nearly filling the valley's floor, as if placed there by an artist named God for sheer, stunning visual relief. Voted one of the most picturesque and romantic places in the world.

The air was cool, clean and crisp, laden with the invigorating scents of pine and juniper. Julia-Rae had been to many incredible, natural places in the world, but none of them took her breath away as the sheer visual glory of Lake Louise did. In all of her years of living in Alberta, she had rarely visited this jewel of the Canadian Rockies.

Julia-Rae had originally planed on hiking around the north side of Lake Louise and visiting the toe of Mt. Victoria's glacier, where the Six Glaciers Teahouse sat. The Canadian Mountain parks brochure stated it was a five-and-a-half-kilometer hike. Her head still buzzed a little from last night's wine, she had one too many glasses with her friend Linda. But she had a blast it had been too long since she had a good laugh and the pleasure of a fine friend for company. During college, where they first met, she and Linda often got together over a bottle of wine. She glanced at her watch and realized by the time she got back it would be well past lunch. "Oh well better late then never," she muttered and started up the paved trail.

The whole scene of the valley before her, wove a spell of natural beauty, Julia-Rae had a hard time restraining herself from wanting to snap a couple dozen pictures. But she wanted to take pictures from an angle different than the usual pictures shot by tourists. Pictures geared to the theme of her magazine. Pictures that an adventurous woman on a hike in Canada's Rockies would feel compelled to take or at least want to visit.

Quickly, the trail that meandered along the right edge of the lake, wound its way into the pine trees. The trail would take her around a rocky outcropping to the very birthplace of this magnificent lake. Lake Louise was rated one of the most romantic places in the world, no small wonder as everything about it was perfect.

The trail wandered in and out of the jack pine forest skirting the edge of the lake.

Everything around her, from the crystal, clear waters to the sentinels of rock towering over her were serenely silent. Yet all of it held voices that called to her, wanting to speak through the aperture of her camera. Eventually Julia-

Rae would talk back to those voices with her camera, until she captured the spirit and essence of this place.

Julia-Rae jumped as something splashed in the water just ahead of her. Perhaps just a fish, she thought at first. Except for one small fact, she knew in a lake this cold fish couldn't exist. A grunt broke the eerie mid-morning quiet. Something was just ahead of her on the path as the trail veered towards the edge of the lake. Great, what if a bear was just ahead of her on the trail, her mind raced. There was hardly anyone else out here. Julia-Rae was just about to retreat, when a male voice broke the stillness.

"Damn, that waters cold!"

Well, it was quiet, she thought. She took a few steps closer and spotted him once she was clear of some of the trees. He stood, just ahead of her, a man clad only in a pair of scandalous white shorts that were stretched too tight over his ample leg muscles and a tan tee-shirt. She pulled free her digital camera and began clicking away. The tee-shirt that she would read later said ‘Bite Me’ on the front side and ‘I did and got Rabies in Banff.’ on the back side. His wet, blonde hair hung in trails against his tanned skin. He looked nearly naked with the wet tee-shirt and shorts clinging to him. She caught the ripple of his muscles as he wrung out his hair. A dark vee crept down the center of his chest and the nice compact pouch of his maleness lay outlined from between his thighs. Yup, I could see where he keeps his sandwiches, as Linda would say. There was only one male crazy enough to go for a dip in a glacier fed lake. Crazy, but sexy, as the morning mist unfolded across the cool still waters of the lake and the sun streamed across the valley, there Roy stood practically naked in his wet clothes. Mists evaporating from him as she took a couple more before walking up.

Cold water dripped down his legs and arms, raising goosebumps she could see from where she stood. “Are you crazy? The water here remains a near constant one degree Celsius."

Roy shivered and shook the water from his loose blonde hair. "Yeah, glacier fed and all that stuff. Wow, she's cold, so much for trying to do a lap around the lake." He grabbed a towel and began drying himself off.

"A lap. . ., you'd most likely go into cold water shock and either have a massive heart attack or freeze to death after about twenty feet." Julia-Rae giggled, men and their macho I-can-do-anything attitudes. He was clearly another case, albeit deliciously wonderful, of testosterone poisoning.

"So we meet again," he shook his head to one side as if trying to dislodge water from his ear. "I think there's a fish stuck in my ear."

"Even fish aren't crazy enough to live in this water and if they did they'd definitely have sweaters on." She said with a smile, "probably your brain frozen into little balls of ice cubes."

He finished drying himself off and stuffed the towel into the handle of a large wicker picnic basket that was sitting beside him. “I’m going on a short hike up the Fairview trail. There’s some great pictures to be taken up there. Care to join me?”

“I’d love to, but I was going to go hiking around the lake to the edge of the glacier and aren’t you going to be a little cold?”

“Nah, the sun will dry me off in no time. Besides, I’ve done that hike around the lake and you’ll get better pictures near sunset. The sun highlights the Chateau and the mountains behind it.”

Julia-Rae thought about it a moment. She hadn’t really anything planned for the afternoon anyway, and as far as she hated to admit it, he knew his lighting angles and was right. So, she had time to do a short hike. The buzz in her head had already begun to clear from too much wine drank last night with Linda.

"So, what do you say?" Roy stepped onto the trail, the skoosh of his runners let her know hadn't taken them off before stepping into the water.

"Don't suppose those are waterproof?"

"Hey, aren't all runners?"

"No, hence the term shoes for running in and not deep seadiving." She laughed. Men.

"Not so smart, but this is. I've got a hot lunch." He held the wicker basket up. A most delicious aroma of something hot from inside wafted towards her.

"Hmmm, smells good, perhaps I'll join you after all, on one condition." Her guts jabbed at her, reminding her she hadn't bothered to grab a half decent breakfast, other than a muffin and coffee, main breakfast of the super woman on the go.

"Name your pleasure, fair maiden."

"I'll go with you on this hike, but you got to go with me on my hike after."

"Let's see either I go wandering off by myself and meet a possible bear. I run off, said bear eats my lunch while I watch. Or I'm forced to go on two hikes with a gorgeous woman- hmm- tough decision. Okay, deal. You probably just want me for my food, I tell ya, the way to a modern-day woman's heart is through her stomach."

Somehow, he must have set this up. A man of surprises and take control, she liked. "Who said anything about working your way into my heart? All you've managed to do for me, so far, is wreck my camera." The harshness of her response disturbed Julia-Rae. He was strangely silent.

"Ah, look I'm sorry, I don't mean to sound like a bitch. Yes, I'll join you. I guess I'm just a little worked up, too much stress at work, I apologize." The truth was she was about to go off on a walk through the woods with a handsome man that was driving her envious with desire.

"Apology accepted; I've been there. Let's see if I can't relieve your stress and with a most pleasant adventurous afternoon. Did you get a bill for the lens? I'll reimburse you when we get back to my hotel room."

"Deal." She didn't like the implication of returning to his hotel room, knowing Roy it would lead to something more devious and intimate.

"Good, shall we follow the yellow brick road then?" Roy held his arm up and let Julia-Rae put her arm into the crook of his. Her cool soft fingers sent a shiver of electricity through him. Every time she touched him it was like being hit by a wave of erotic longing. He didn't hunger after many women, but if he did, she'd reside under door number one, number two and number three.

He remembered the feeling the flow of her curves pressed against him at the bungie jump. It was all he could do not to want to kiss her, like he wanted to do right now. Roy shook his head. Remember lover boy, you're only here to seduce this girl and help persuade her to sign over her business, he thought to himself. Yet there was so much of this bold and brassy woman that he enjoyed. She was so much like Carrie. He closed his eyes for a moment, fighting not to go there in his mind. Memories he wasn't prepared to dredge up yet, nor wanted to at this moment.

Later In the early evening they began to walk down the hiking trail together, the trailhead to Mt. Fairview was back beside the parking lot left to the hotel. His very nearness seemed to cut through the crispness of the mountain air. She caught a whiff of his earthy cologne; it was mixed with the smell of a clean-shaven man. That wonderful smell of aftershave, earthiness, was so ruggedly masculine. It reminded her of getting up every morning as a child and watching her dad use a straight razor to shave. Of how she'd run her fingers over his face when he was done, to see just how smooth a cut he had achieved. Julia-Rae wanted to do more then run her hands over Roy's face, she wanted to run her hands over his body. To feel the hardness of his body.

His muscular strength, holding her, thrusting into her. . . Damn, I'm slipping into fantasy overload.

"You okay?"

"Yeah, must be the clean air out here, it's just a little too heady for me. I guess I'm just used to breathing photographic odors and the car fumes of the city." She was too embarrassed to say anything about last night's episode.

"Yeah, I know what you mean on that one."

Julia-Rae felt a bit of an ache in her head, the last fighting remnants from last nights carousing with Linda, but then what were good friends are for. Roy had intuitively put his arm out and she curled hers around it walking arm in arm. Never had she wanted to seek the strong comfort of a male's arm, to bury herself in the strength that flowed through his body. It seemed the most natural thing in the world to be walking with him beside her like this, the thought comforting and terrifying at the same time. Julia-Rae pressed her fingers into the hardness of his arm. To have that hardness pressed up against her like back at Machu Picchu or at the bungie jump. Julia-Rae quivered. What would it feel like to surrender to this man? Feel his hardness, driving into her, driving her over that edge, that wonderfully delicious edge. Somehow she knew in her heart that a man of such off the wall craziness would have no problem driving her insanely wild. Or was it her that was becoming insanely wild? And that was the problem wasn't it. All she was beginning to do around him was think about kissing those tight lips. To feel his hands caressing her breasts, his hot mouth on her aroused nipples, teasing her, exciting her. How was she supposed to be concentrating on work when they're at the most romantic place in North America, walking arm in arm with a hunk of a mysterious man. Yes, girl, think of those pictures you want to take. As they hiked through the woods she kept trying to stay conscious of camera angles and camera shots.

As the trail steepened and narrowed, he chose to walk in front of her. Each movement of those strong legs, the cords of his muscles flexing and the flex of his rear as he climbed up the trail sent a delicious quiver through her. The only pictures she truly wanted to take were of him naked holding her in his arms, shivers racing through them as they stood knee deep in the frigid waters of the lake.

She smiled, recalling the one time she got in trouble at her grandma's house. She was twelve and had gone skinny-dipping with Richard, a friend of hers, who also happened to be a boy. Up until that point of her life, other than the fact that kissing boys would give you monkey germs, there wasn't a whole lot of difference between boyfriends and girlfriends. Her grandma gave her supreme hell, not that she listened much at that age. It was the first time she became conscious of the difference between her body and a boys. She remembered peeling her clothes off and Richard gawking at the stubble growing between her legs, while his body had not quite begun to change yet. Or as her grandma related to her, "You best be careful Julia-Rae, the boys will want to be doing more than just playing dinky toys with you now."

"Here looks as good a spot as any, what do you think?"

"Sure, it's wonderful." Julia-Rae stared out across the valley. The TransCanada highway wound its way like a minute silver thread through the valley. Tiny multi-colored specks of automobiles that looked like ants from this distance, glittered along the highway below.

Roy flung the blanket across the meadow grass. Both were sweating after the short but very invigorating hike, which had cut across the flanks of Mt. Fairview. They camped in a small vee that was devoid of trees. The head of the valley took them over the side to Paradise Valley below. Julia-Rae had taken some inspiring pictures of the valley, Moraine Lake in the distance and the Valley of the Ten Peaks. They had then retreated to this, the sunlit side of the trail to relax.

“Well, it was a little tough, but at least there’s more air here then in Machu Picchu,” Roy gasped. “Fortunately, not quite as high up.”

Julia-Rae had long ago stripped down to her jogging shorts and tee-shirt. Sweat ran down her back forming wet splotches on both sides of her upper body.

Roy glanced at her and then at the Bow valley spread out before them. “Incredible view, I always find it amazing how one can hike up only a couple of kilometers and see something as awe inspiring as this.”

In fact there were only a couple of traces of civilization in the densely treed valley. One was the green clad ski slopes of Whitehorn Mountain, where the Lake Louise ski runs where located. Even laden with summer grass on all of its runs the summit still had patches of snow that remained year-round. The other trace of man’s encroachment to this valley and the only way in or out of this nearly pristine wilderness was the TransCanada highway glittering below.

"Well, was it worth it?"

"Yes, it was. I got quite a few pictures on the backside, of Moraine Lake and the Valley of the Ten Peaks. I didn't know that was the same valley on back of the old twenty-dollar Canadian bills from the sixties." Roy shook his head a little, he had more knowledge about this area than she realized.

"Good, then this hike was perhaps just the right thing for you." Roy stared at Julia-Rae. Clad in only a tee-shirt and jogging shorts she looked incredible.

"Yeah, that and wrecking my figure."

Roy had more then noticed her figure. He noticed the curve of her hips and the fact her breasts while ample but not overly large, sat nice and high on her body. That she wore only a sport bra and he could see her nipples getting hard every once in a while when a cool breeze stirred the crisp mountain air. In fact, he found it hard to not ogle at her and once nearly fell off the trail he had been staring so hard.

Always keep an eye on your feet and on the trail he'd been told years ago by an experienced hiker, easier said than done when there's a vivacious redhead walking in front of you with nearly nothing on. Roy wiped an annoying bead of sweat from his brow and smiled. "If that is your idea of a wrecked figure, I'd love to see what you looked like before."

Julia-Rae blushed. Somehow his appraisal of her figure seemed genuine, not at all like the wolf stares she often got from men.

"Okay, it's lunch time," he said breaking the awkwardness of the moment. The tantalizing aroma of barbecued chicken along with fresh sourdough bagels filled the air.

Julia-Rae's stomach growled in response. She was hungrier then she thought, the hike had stirred up a appetite that normally didn't like eating anything in the morning.

Roy quickly spread out a feast before them. It included a tossed salad, a hearty helping of trail mix, cut up cantaloupe and honeydew melon for dessert. He had two kinds of sandwiches on toasted bagels. One set of bagels had smoked salmon and artichoke cream cheese and the other, "my favorite, crunchy peanut butter and raspberry bagels." Roy said, waving at the food before them.

Julia-Rae reached for the peanut butter bagels.

"Hey," he said, "those are for me."

"Oh I thought you brought them for me."

"They're my favorite." Both blurted out at the same time and laughed.

Roy then pulled out two bottles of chilled white wine, a pair of long-stemmed wineglasses with elegant black bases and a red rose in a thin vase. "If you care to partake, I don't drink alcohol."

Sure enough, Julia-Rae looked at the two bottles, one was a bottle of Pia Dor and the other was a bottle of Chardonnay. The label on the bottle of chardonnay read, with the alcohol tastefully removed. "Why don't you drink alcohol?"

"It's a long story that I don't want to get into right now. Suffice to say it caused me a great deal of grief in the past." Roy's face bore a grim look.

Something dark and sinister from his past swam in his eyes. She would ask later, now was not the time. Feeling it prudent to change the subject Julia-Rae said, "I see you were not planning on dining alone." She sat down next to him. Julia-Rae watched the cords on his forearms as he effortlessly twisted the corkscrew into one of the bottles of wine. There wasn't much about him she hadn't watched on the way up here. The man definitely worked out. The taunt cords of his solidly muscular legs. Legs she'd love to have twined around hers. What was is it Linda had said she found nothing sexier than the smell of a sweaty worked up man. Julia-Rae had to admit that musky odor emanating from his body, was enticingly sexy.

"Yeah, well, I was hoping on meeting up with you before setting out on this hike. So I had the hotel make me a lunch for two. It definitely looks better then the Chinese food I had last night in

Calgary."

Julia-Rae frowned, he had reminded her of the problem of what to do with her Hong Kong pictures.

"Ah, judging by the look on your face either I just said something wrong or my twenty-four-hour Right Guard just expired." The last of the corks came free with a resounding pop that echoed away into the distance.

"No, when you mentioned Chinese food, it reminded me of a project I was working on. I just found out that the majority of my Hong Kong pictures got overexposed somehow. Probably those photo detectors at the airport. Anyways I don't know if I've got enough pictures left to do a good expose."

"Hong Kong, you say. As a matter of fact I did a photo shoot on Hong Kong late last year and got some great pictures. You'd be welcome to see them and if you can use some then great. But you must promise me one thing."

"And what is that."

"I send you the pictures and you promise not to talk anymore about work, deal. Besides, the mention of work is beginning to break the mood."

"Deal, oh really, my, you are a sweet man." Julia-Rae smiled as he handed her a wine glass and began pouring her some of the wine. She didn't really expect to use any of his pictures, but at least he was kind enough to offer.

"Shh, don't say it too loud. We'll have every tacky dressed tourist flocking here this side of the Rockies."

Julia-Rae giggled as she sipped on the wine. There was one thing about Roy she really liked. He had a way of making her laugh. It flowed out of him so naturally. "Do you hike much?" She knew his answer even before she asked.

The flex of the muscles in his leg gave him away. The only thing she really wanted him to do was to reach over and kiss her.

"I'm always amazed how one can walk up only a couple of K's and see something as wonderful as this view. Being a freelance photographer, I've traveled to lots of places and often had to hike into some remote areas. But I don't do a whole lot of hiking for the sake of hiking, but in the end, yes, I do a lot of hiking. So, if that round about answer works."

She stared out across the valley painfully aware of just how close he was sitting to her and how quickly the wine was hitting her. Maybe it was the heat or the lack of food in her stomach. "Yes, I know exactly what you mean. I've clamored over a few rocks and worn trails myself." A kink in her leg forced her to stand up. His eyes seemed to always be watching her. She knew he liked what he saw. Did he feel the same intoxicating energy she did? Did he want to crush her in his arms as badly as she wanted him to? Did he want to feel her naked body against his, like she did? Julia-Rae rose and left the entire mountainside as a wave of dizziness washed away reality.

Chapter Five

"Are you okay?" His voice pulled her back from a black swimming haze.

"What happened?" Julia-Rae said as she opened her eyes and looked into Roy's concerned face. His eyes of deep blue, comforting and somehow grounding.

"You stood up and promptly fell over. I managed to catch you before you tumbled down the mountain."

Roy spoke with a look of concern on his face. The heat of his body sent a fascinating shiver through her as he held her.

"Yes, I'm fine, I think," she gasped fighting to stay conscious as the world did a slow pirouette around her as she held his eyes in her vision. "Perhaps the wine wasn't a good idea before eating and after the workout from hiking. Were you worried?" If he wasn't, Julia-Rae knew she was, the wine was definitely lowering her resistance and adding to the desire building inside of her.

"Actually yes, I was wondering how I'd fit you in this lunch basket and carry you off this mountain."

"You'd carry me off this mountain?" The idea seemed rather chivalrous to Julia-Rae. Those dark pits of blue smiled at her and she knew if he had to, he would carry her single-handedly off the mountain. Those dark pits of blue beckoned. The intensity of his eyes blazing like a coral reef blue blending into a background of sand washed beach. Yet somewhere lost in the depths of those passionate tropical waters circled something as dangerous as the sharks that inhabit those serene tropical reefs.

In the background the meadow grasses stirred in delightful repose from the warmth of the sun's gaze and trickles of water, giggling away in impish delight, from slowly vanishing patches of snow. That and only the sound of their breathing stirred the air, as he drew nearer. He stopped just fractions of an inch from her face. The warmth of his breath sent shivers through Julia-Rae. The heat radiating from those lips sent shock waves of sensual electricity through her. Kiss me now, she wanted to whisper and as if answering that silent command, he did.

An electrifying pulse of erotic energy like being dipped naked into ice water on a hot day, surged through Julia-Rae as he softly brushed his lips against hers. Those hard lips surrounded by prickles of harsh stubble that threatened to tear at the delicateness of her skin as he rubbed against her. It was the most erotic sensual thing anyone had ever done to her. Julia-Rae reached up and pulled Roy to her. On his lips the taste of fresh mountain air. Her breath filled of strong woodsy male cologne mixed with the musky sweat that was undeniably Roy Sutter. She needed him, wanted him, nothing else mattered, unleashing a dam of suppression.

Gone was the mountainside, gone was the seething intense blue sky. Only the hot crush of his lips mattered. Lips that sent fire to parts of her body Julia-Rae had denied any feelings to for a long time, his tongue stole at hers. A fire that tore all shambles of sanity from her ripped her free from all of her reality and left her poised on the edge of a precarious precipice, teetering. Floodgates of deep sultry desire hammered at her and sucked her down its swirling mysterious waters.

He pulled away for a moment. Julia-Rae opened her eyes. “Oh God,” she moaned. Julia-Rae realized she was shaking. Shaking from the hunger of wanting more and shaking from the fear of where he’d take her and what he’d do to her once he got her there.

The hardness, the heat of his maleness she felt pressed against her as he held her. The strength with which he held her. In his eyes Julia-Rae saw the fierce passions raging, he reminded her of a warrior, returning home after a long absence, desirous, yet wary. As the sun beat down Julia-Rae knew that he too had been sucked down a pathway of emotional craving. The hardness in his arms. Cravings of long suppressed hunger raging unabated in his soul. The warrior claiming his rights, his lady. All that she saw in those hazy swirls of blue. He wanted her as badly as she did him.

"I-I," Roy tried to speak.

She was afraid his words, any words, would shatter the sensual web they begun to weave around each other. The heat of his hardness seemed to throb in response. How she wanted him to be inside of her, driving her into a forgotten world of erotic passions. She felt her own response, her own wetness calling to him, needing him demanding him; beginning the ancient throbbing dance of lovers. What was it about him that impassioned her so, or was it simply that she had been so long denied any physical pleasure for herself?

Julia-Rae put her arms around his neck and pulled his lips to hers. They kissed like hungry dogs, unleashing damning passions. Parting the veil of her lips she pushed him back against the blanket. The stab of his hot wet tongue sent cascades of hunger and desire throbbing through her. A deep lusty moan escaped her throat, she wanted more. They kissed until she couldn't stand it anymore. His tongue exploring her mouth, as she lay on top of him.

His warm hands shook as they ran down her sides and pulled her top free from the confining waistband of her jogging shorts. Julia-Rae moaned again as his hands touched her skin and ran along her back until they reached her bra. She had only donned a sport bra this morning and it offered little resistance as his hands stole underneath, cupping her hot breasts.

Julia-Rae reached around and pulled her top over her head. She wanted, needed to have her breasts free. They begged him to run his hands over them, to crush them against the hardness of his naked chest, fell the heat of his mouth on them. The cool mountain air sent a sobering wave of aliveness through her as she pulled her bra hastily over her head. His eyes opened in response and a moan escaped his lips. Every tender nearly invisible hair on her breasts stood aroused as his hands ever so lightly ran across the surface of her breasts. Not cupping them, not holding them but just skimming across the surface, with the back of his hands, exciting her even more. His hands were touching, dancing with each aroused hair on her breasts. Julia-Rae moaned again and pressed his hands against her breasts. She reached down and inadvertently touched his hardness. It pulsed with heat. Then she did something she had never done before. Through the material that threatened to burst, Julia-Rae gently caressed him.

He shuddered with a moan putting his hand over hers. “Don’t, I’ll explode any second now if you continue.” No, she wanted him inside of her, exploding inside of her, driving her over that edge of ecstasy.

The sobering sound of voices broke the air. Strangers coming up the trail. Julia-Rae and Roy both stopped and in unison turned their heads to listen. "Damn," escaped their lips as their impassioned tableau was broken.

Julia-Rae's mind scrambled back to the land of reality. She scrambled to regain some sort of decency before the voices materialized into real people. Perhaps it was a good thing someone else showed up to pull her head straight again, back from that land of insanity and deep soulful passions. Neither spoke at first as they hurriedly packed. Julia-Rae's hands shook, her legs trembled with desire. The kind of desire that painfully and slowly subsided from unquenched hunger, leaving an unfulfilled wetness calling to him.

"Time to go, I'm afraid," he finally crocked. He seemed to be as much in a hurry to leave as she was. Sanity returning to both.

Julia-Rae remained silent, unable to talk as her insides shook trying to quell the madness that sang within to the innermost passionate cravings of her soul, crying to be released to the unfettered winds. This man was more then just dangerous, all right. He was also delicious and as excited as her. A very deadly combination.

Silently they composed themselves and began the journey back down to the hotel. Roy was strangely quiet. Maybe part of her knew that he too was questioning what had begun to happen up there, just now. Never had a man's lips elicited such passion from her. Never even close. Perhaps he was shocked by her vivacious response to his kiss.

"Ah look, I'm a sorry. I uh- don't normally go around attacking a man after he kisses me." Somehow, she needed to say something in order to get her confused mind into some semblance of order. Some kind of justification for her actions.

Coming up the trail a trio of hikers waved to them.

"Don't be," he gasped, "I've always loved a woman of intensity and fire. I, ah, just guess I didn't expect it from you. Caught me off guard."

God, now he probably thinks I'm some sort of sex starved nymph. "It's okay really, I just need to get back to the hotel. I promised someone I'd give them a phone call." Both of them knew that was a lie. "Can we do supper tonight?"

"I, a. . ." she didn't know what to say.

"Just supper and a relaxing hike around the lake, nothing else. I did promise to take you on a hike around the lake. Besides that's the best time to take some shots of the chateau, with the setting sun bouncing off the brick walls."

They quickly entered the canopy of pines and stunted cedars. Only a few bent blades of grass remained to mark their passage. That and a faint lingering aroma of passion. From somewhere came a lonely sighing wind to rustle the mountainside and dispel the hints of passion on wings of invisible gossamer. As the winds had done forever, spiriting amongst the pines of unknown age. His words painting a gorgeous picture in her mind.

"Okay," Julia-Rae said relenting. She wanted to get to know this man this strange enigmatic man called Roy Sutter. Get to know him and let him into her heart. Still, the thought of her almost attacking him stunned her. Was that really what she was like, aggressive and dominating or was this simply a measure of how much desire she had for this man. Let him in, hell he'd already walked into places in her heart she'd never let anyone enter before. The long, stark white fingers of fear sunk their way into the tender corridors of her heart. It's okay, she thought. Let him in, he won't hurt me. A tremble shook inside.

Chapter Six

Julia-Rae had dressed in a long flowing, black satin dress. The back cut too low and the fabric was too sheer for her liking. Her breasts threatened to pop out as Roy seated her at the dinner table. The dress was Linda's and the only one that she had that Julia-Rae thought would fit. Since Linda was just slightly smaller and less developed than Julia-Rae, she tended to wear dresses that helped accent a bust-line Julia-Rae didn't need any help in. It did do one thing though and that was to get Roy's attention, not that his mind was wondering from her whenever they were together. His eyes tried not to wonder over the flesh spilling out. She smiled, liking the temptations plaguing him.

"Care to order, sir?" Linda said as she walked up, her name tag read, Denise. Julia-Rae tried to suppress a giggle. Linda was dressed up in a waitress uniform, although about two sizes too small. She was wearing a push up bra that also threatened to spill everything out. It was her idea to tease Roy and serve them tonight. She wanted to see if he really was interested more in Julia-Rae. Roy sat across from her, looking very handsome in a black suit and deep green vested shirt. He suited it looking right at home in the formal attire. He looked quite commanding, Julia-Rae could see him looking very comfortable in a business suit. It was the first time she had seen him in anything other than something casual. Other than the tuxedo at the bungie jump and he was divine in that outfit. He looked very comfortable dressed up, like he could easily lead a business meeting or be the president of some corporation. Unusual for a man that seemed to thrive on old jeans and tee-shirts.

"Oh, I haven't really decided what I would like." Roy responded.

Linda moved around to Roy's side of the table and bent over as low as she could go without spilling her cleavage all over Roy. "Here let me assist you, sir."

Julia-Rae flipped up the menu and buried her face behind it, at least to hide her smirk that she struggled to contain. Linda was about as adventurous and rambunctious as Julia-Rae, although she tended to be a little more on the risqué side.

"Could I suggest the tender turkey breasts, dipped in a red wine sauce and smothered with a creamy dill coating?" She purred seductively.

Roy took one quick glance at Julia-Rae, his eyes breathed fire. "No, actually, I'll go for the stuffed sweet red bell peppers."

Linda straightened up. "Excellent choice sir. The red peppers are very ripe tonight and extremely full-bodied. I'm sure you won't be disappointed by your choice."

"Let's say I'm starting to develop a craving for full-bodied, aromatic reds. Thank you."

"And you Ms. or is it Mrs.?"

"It's definitely Ms. and I'll have the same as him, the gentleman has definitely very good taste and is an excellent judge of character." She winked slightly at Roy.

"Yes, I can see he definitely has his stomach set on the main course set before him, I'll be right back with the wine."

Linda politely grabbed the two menus and winked mischievously at Julia-Rae. One thing Julia-Rae could see this man had eyes for only one female form in this room and it was sitting at the table across from him. A shudder swept through her. She still tasted the chill of the mountain air on his lips, the sweat of the hike and his desire. Never had she hungered to be in a man's arms like she had done this afternoon. Her, the self-confident career woman, who could only think of sinking into the safe rapture of his strong arms.

If those hikers hadn't come up the trail she'd have made love to Roy. Made love to him, no she'd virtually attacked him. Was this what it was like to want someone, to let someone get close and get inside of you? Julia-Rae smiled at Roy; she was eternally grateful for the timing of those hikers. Nothing in life was coincidence she'd been told long ago. Everything happens for a reason. Julia-Rae wanted to keep him at a safe distance, she had to know he was okay, he wasn't out to hurt her and that she could trust him, even though her body was crying out to let him in.

That was a problem, wasn't it? The urge to say something rude and shove him away was strong. Use that temper of hers and push him out of her life. A realization hit her just then, she'd done that before, got angry and pushed people out of her life. Kept men from entering and hurting her like she'd been hurt before. Julia-Rae wanted to run, run to the safety of her condo, of her job, of her solitary existence. Run back to her lonely life. At least it was safe there. There she didn't need anyone else and there was no one to hurt her.

"You're awfully quiet all of a sudden. Did I say anything wrong?" Roy said looking concerned.

"No, it's just, ah, my dress, I'm a little self-conscious, I haven't gone out dressed like this in a long time, feeling a little overexposed." She couldn't say what she was really thinking and yet it wasn't far from the truth, she hadn't dressed up in a long time. She pulled the material up trying to hide part of her ample cleavage.

"Speaking of needing to cover-up, don't you think the waitress is being rather forward tonight?"

"Forward, where do you get the old English phrases from? And yes, she is being very forward. If she keeps it up I'll be asking the manager to have a talk with her, her behavior is bordering on the edge of being unacceptable in an establishment like this." "You wouldn't Roy." She gasped.

"Yes, I would. I've run a business before and know how important feedback on my staff is from my customers."

Julia-Rae had never thought of it before, but she could see Roy as a boss running a company. Probably why he carried himself with such confidence, even in that suit. "I got my afflicted old English words from my prim and proper and very English grandmother, Grace. My mother died from complications shortly after I was born. Grace did a lot of the parental duties when my dad wasn't around. Dad ran an accounting business. Even though I was his only child and he loved me dearly, his business kept him working late many a night."

"Did he ever remarry?"

"No, dad said it tore too much out of him to do that. Running his business and looking after me became his whole life." Roy's face sagged a little, shriveling.

"You okay, did I say anything wrong?"

"No, it just that I can relate to your dad. Running a business is a twelve hour a day affair only to come home and do two hours more of paperwork. I did that for a number of years. In the end I had a good offer and sold. I did well and began to do what I always wanted to do, become a freelance photographer. I've been happy with my life ever since."

Roy seemed very low key while he talked. Perhaps it was just the hike, she thought, but he didn't sound like someone happy with his life. His eyes bore a distant and at the same time a hard and merciless look. There was more to ask about at a later date.

Roy ordered the meals, as Linda returned. She let him order for her, as her grandmother told her was customary for a proper gentleman to do. Only was it proper for a gentleman to try to seduce her on a mountain trail? Who was she trying to kid? It was her that nearly ripped his clothes off. It was her that wanted him naked on top of her. Julia-Rae adjusted her dress again and motioned to Linda. "Waitress can I have another glass of water, I believe it's definitely getting too hot in here." She winked at Linda and gave her that slight, can it before you get us into trouble look, they were so used to giving each other in college.

"Do you enjoy running your own business?" He asked.

"Yes I do, although it has a lot of challenging moments and I like challenge, but" she stopped for a second, wanting to say…

"And lonely sometimes I bet," he said as if reading her thoughts.

Julia-Rae looked up, "yes it is definitely lonely sometimes." Just how much hadn't really dawned on her until just now. "The loneliness I can handle, I've grown quite used to being on my own, after all as my friend Linda who's quite spiritual once told me I'm the only person I'm ever going to have in my own life, I need to make myself happy. Dad has offered to me a position in his accounting firm and I know some day when he decides to retire he'd like me to take over, but accounting and numbers just isn't my idea of doing life. I really enjoy getting out meeting people and going to adventurous places, I guess doing different things, instead of the same old, same old, is something that I look forward to." Julia-Rae paused giving thought to his comment. "Linda, my best friend, asked me one time too, to get in touch with what I really got out of running my own business. I know for me it boils down to pride of command and being in control of my own destiny." As she talked Julia-Rae noticed that Roy was strangely silent, he had a look that crossed his face of subtle sadness for a brief moment.

"Had the idea of settling down ever occurred to you?" He asked breaking out of that spell that her words had drawn him into. It was nice, she thought, to be candid and honest, just chatting back and forth.

What would life be like as his wife? No grind of having to go to work. Would she like to be at home, raising babies? Unlikely, still the thought of having him to come home to left a scratch down the length of her heart. "But I know someday a man will come along to sweep me off my feet."

"And what if he comes calling and doesn't carry a broom?" Roy asked staring intently into her eyes. Those blue wells of his eyes melting away her soft reserve. He had eyes that could charm the dress off Queen Elizabeth, Julia-Rae snickered to herself. It was one of her grandmother's favorite lines. "Well, in this day and age he'd best be carrying a dust buster," she laughed.

"I've got to admit it's been a long time for me also since I've had anyone in my life. In my line of work I've run into my fair share of ladies and the occasional date has been fun, but none that make me feel like I do around you, Julia-Rae."

He stunned her. Julia-Rae picked up her glass of wine and took a healthy sip and had to ask. “And how do I make you feel?”

“Something I never thought I’d feel again. Giddy, little boy giddy.” He smiled all the way to the corners of those eyes that belonged to the heart of a rugged loner. One she wanted to turn to hers and steal away, lock it up and throw away the key.

Supper had been followed by a very rich chocolate mousse for dessert. It had been better then wonderful, it had been exquisite, but what else could one expect at the Chateau Lake Louise, the number one hotspot for romance in North America. It had given Julia-Rae a great deal of incentive to write her next article. After supper, as agreed they had taken a leisurely stroll around the lake. Talking of small things, avoiding what was really bugging her and perhaps him, she knew. The tension between them was incredible, every time he held her hand or stared into her eyes she wanted to melt away. Melt away to flow beside him in the desire they both felt compelled to complete on what they started earlier on the mountaintop. Hungers awakened in both, aching inside.

He had been every inch the gentleman, not making any advances as they sauntered in and out of the trees. She was sure he'd try something, he didn't. As they had walked he held her arm in his. Each touch of his was like having a bank of cold-water jets spraying her feverish body. Cooling her, yet raising the pressure of her passions. Coming here was not a good thing to do, she realized. Get your article together and get home girl, she thought. This is dangerous unfamiliar territory. Territory he seemed so comfortable with and that was part of the problem. He was too good, too smooth. The man had a die-hard romantic soul. The kind of man most women would kill to have in their lives. So, what was he doing here with her? And why did she want to run? Perhaps it was just her natural cynical nature? As a businesswoman she learned early on, ask questions and lots of them, if you want to get ahead and survive. Still as they walked back through the sumptuous foyer and up the stairs to her room she wanted so hard to give in to the fantasy. To let him in to her heart, only could she afford to?

Roy stood behind her as she looked for her key to get into her hotel room. "Thanks for the hike today and for supper both were excellent."

"My pleasure, shall I step inside and join you for a drink before retiring."

That was an all out lie, she knew he didn't drink. There was only one reason he'd want to be in her room, the same reason she'd want him. "I'd love to Roy, but I have to get an early start on the drive back to Edmonton." Julia-Rae faked a yawn. The truth was she was really afraid of letting him in. The wine from dinner had lowered her resistance, about the same as that drink on the mountain trail and she knew what happened there. No letting him in would lead to only one thing as this afternoon on the mountain had proved.

What was it about him that light brush fires across her? Fires that she didn't want put out. The mere thought of him naked. . . Julia-Rae shook her head. I'm doing it again, letting my emotions run rampant. No, she had to get to know him a little more first. Had to make sure she could handle letting him in, getting that close to her. Trusting him.

"Well then, can we plan a dinner at my condo?"

"Yes, I'd like that. Another evening to relax, take our time and get to know each other some more." Before ripping my clothes off and letting you have your way with me, she thought. An ancient hunger and throb was calling to him, only him, to extinguish. Thank God, he hadn't pressed and tried to come in to her room. Would she be able to resist him, did she want to?

"Are you sure you're not afraid of letting me in?" His voice, slow and measured, lowered in tone. An undercoating of dark, residing hunger lay with each half-whispered syllable. He stepped closer. Julia-Rae felt the heat of his breath on her neck. His words flickered in her ear, enticing her, inciting the pressure pulsing in her blood. Awakening the desires still unquenched within her as she struggled to insert the door key card.

Don't do this Roy, she wanted to cry out. Her heart pounding. Maybe she had thought too soon that he'd not try something like this, that he was a gentleman and not some rebellious loner. "No," she spoke, barely above a whisper. Her hand shook as she pulled the card from her door, the light green to enter. She held the doorknob for support knees growing weak. The strong woodsy scent of his cologne washed over her shoulders like mist curving around a mountain. Cutting her off from the rest of the world, isolating her, possessing her and seducing her with his ethereal energy. Jolts of electricity flashed across her as he breathed on her neck. His very closeness, electrifying. The heat of his body, so close.

"Maybe it's just that I'm afraid of my own desires, it has been a long time for me Roy, a long time without a man in my life. I'm afraid of letting you in."

"So are you afraid then of the passions this man or any man might arouse in you?"

He was standing so close to her if they hadn't any clothes on the ends of their hairs would be touching each other. That thought sent a shudder through her. She held the doorknob tighter. The coolness of the metal pulling Julia-Rae back from that world of heated desires she began to dip into, sobering her.

"No, no man could arouse any deep passions if I didn't want him to." Yes, she thought, say those words and try to believe them. Try to honestly believe them, try to honestly believe yourself. Lying bitch.

Without a word Roy gently but firmly pressed her to the door. Julia-Rae felt the hard crush of his body, his desire hot against her backside. The feel of her rear pressed up against him inciting the most carnal of thoughts. With one hand he brushed her curls across and ran the tip of his tongue along the exposed delicate hairs on the nape of her neck. Teasing, hungry, all her world centered on that wickedly, wet tongue licking slowly at her ear. His breath quick, passionate, wanting. Each lick ripping away at her defenses until only the raw relinquished desire of earlier, on the mountain, crawled over her with a savage hunger. Too long buried, too long hidden away. Julia-Rae moaned. Both of her palms were now pressed against the wooden door, clutching at it, trying to hold onto something, anything; as her world of senses erupted in insatiable yearning. If she had nails long enough, they'd be digging into the wood, like she wanted to be digging into his back as he possessed her. That ache, that deep throbbing want for him had begun again just like back on that mountain. Except this time, it didn't have to build, it was there like a full-blown tornado, claiming all of her senses in an epidemic collapse of her defenses.

Only the firm press of his body kept her from falling over. Let him run his hands over my body, she thought wildly, let him pull my clothes slowly away from me. Here and now. She knew she was growing damp in that place that hungered the most for him. The place she needed him to enter, even as they were positioned, then and there.

Roy let go of her hair and whispered the truth into her ear. "Tell me Julia-Rae, tell me if I haven't raised any deep passion within you. Tell me." He paused his breath short, "or better yet tell yourself."

Her heart pounded until it drummed in her ears. The truth, he knew the truth as she did herself.

"Yes," she first whispered to herself, then softly out loud, "yes I want you more then anything I've ever wanted in my life."

Silence and coolness brought Julia-Rae back from that doorway of desire Roy had thrust aside. Only cool air answered the deep sexual throb from her midsection.

She hadn't even noticed he'd left, like a silently stalking cougar through the underbrush. Only a residue of his cologne and the wetness of his tongue remained evaporating on the air, inciting her. Julia-Rae shook as she opened her door.

Locking the door behind her, she flung herself onto her bed. Staring at the blank wall before her. Her body ached like a migraine gone bad and wetness seeped from her. She touched herself, where she needed him, something she normally never did. She was throbbing, wanting and craving Roy. What was it about him that set every fiber of her being on edge and turned her world upside down, where rationality ended and lust unfulfilled hunger began. Carnal cravings for him she never had before, for him or any man. She pulled the top cover over herself as she turned and wrapped herself in the warmth and security of the blanket.

That was how she remained clutching sheets in her dress, until the wake-up call startled her back to reality the next morning.

On Monday Julia-Rae dialed Linda from her office, she wanted to thank her for asking her to come out there on the weekend, sorry she didn't see her as she checked out.

Her office overflowed in the heady richness of dozens of red roses. The earthly, sensuous fragrance, of the flowers, filled the entire office. "Hi, how's it going?"

"Great, life with you."

"Well let's just say I'm sitting here in my office surrounded by red roses, four dozen at least, I've a pile of Hong Kong pictures courtesy of a Roy Sutter on my desk like he promised to send and a card. The card says, thanks for the wonderfully engaging weekend see you Saturday night 7:00, my place number four Le Marchand Place."

"Wow, you must have really put him on his ear. The man checked out early in the morning Sunday well before I was up and on duty. I was a little worried, he never even said goodbye to you I'll bet. What you do to him lady?"

"Ah, that's the problem, other than kiss on the mountain top and starting some heavy petting before a family came marching up the trail, nothing. I don't get it Linda, what is it about me that excites him."

"Well, have you looked in the mirror lately, girl you've got the curves I only wish I could possess."

"Linda, I'll be honest, I'm scared silly, I've never been this, ah, how can I say?"

"How about worked up."

"Exactly, this worked up about a guy. I nearly attacked him on that trail, if those hikers hadn't arrived I'd, I'd. . ."

"I'd what? Been making sweet, delicious love? Well girl, I know you've been keeping yourself locked up the last few years, but isn't that what enjoying life is all about?"

Julia-Rae paused, making love, the words hit her with the clarity of a two by four across the forehead. "No, it can't be. I mean I just met the guy, he's rude, arrogant, runs around like some crazy teenager strung out on testosterone and. . ."

"And he's driving you wild, it shows Julia-Rae, it shows. Hey gotta go, give me a call sometime and anytime you want to come on out call me. You never know when I can book the honeymooners suite for you, it's got a great hot tub."

"Thanks Linda."

Julia-Rae hung up the phone. In love? Was this what being in love was like, the heady and insanely intense emotions that surged through her every time he got near or even when she thought about him. Was this how her dad felt about her mom? Is this why he never remarried? Julia-Rae pushed aside the package of pictures and picked up the card. To be alone at his place. A shot of electricity ran through her. She'd be completely on his territory and he definitely was the type to use that to his advantage, if she didn't. Roy wasn't home when she called so she left a message on his answering machine. His voice sounded deep and challenging on the recorded message. She would be there, she only hoped she was up to the challenge.

Chapter Seven

"Good to see you again Mr. Sutter," said the matronly, dark-haired nurse on duty at the reception desk as Roy strode into the Lendrum Nursing Home.

"Has the check arrived to look after the yearly bill?" He knew it had, Antonio had taken care of it, just like he took care of virtually everything else needed to run the office whenever Roy wasn't around.

"Yes, Mrs. Hill instructed me to tell you that everything is fine and the tax receipts have been forwarded to your Vancouver address as requested. Now I suppose you're here to see your son."

"Thanks Mrs. Sanderson, yes I've only a couple of hours to spare before leaving on business." The business of seducing gorgeous woman, he thought. "But I wanted to stop by and see him."

Mrs. Sanderson reached over and hit the buzzer to open the door. Roy thought it funny that in all the years of him coming here they hadn't said more to each other than a few precursory words. Words needed in order for him to get inside and see his son. As Roy entered, he spied the new nametag perched on the receptionists impeccably attired uniform. It had been changed from Mrs. Sanderson to read Eveline Sanderson. It never donned on him that she might have a first name. Did that also mean that she was no longer married?

"Well, I must admit, Mr. Sutter, you don't often stay long but, after all of these years you still come a least once every other week."

Roy paused in the doorway. "Well after all, he's still my son," Roy muttered, not trying to sound miffed at her remarks. It dawned on him that she didn't know his first name. "And it's Roy, Eveline." Roy had a habit of always reading name tags and calling everyone by their first name, when he knew it. Eveline smiled as Roy walked past her.

The sterility of the corridors filled his lungs. Corridors rank with pine scents of Lysol scrubbed on them daily. This nursing home was probably no different than any other. It was a place where old people came to spend the last remaining part of their lives, to whither away and rot. Several old people sat in chairs lining the walls. For some hands shook as they sat, some their heads, some both. Others sat with a blank look on their face. "Alive in their bodies and little else," he muttered. Bodies that were mere shells betraying their fragile commitment of time left on this earth.

Perhaps that was why he enjoyed spending time with Mrs. Leighton, she was one of the few that was still sharp as a whip. Roy had debated many times with her trying to get her into a care facility. When he saw some of the people that lived here he wondered whether that would be wise. From around the corner he heard a commotion. Someone was yelling and putting up a fuss. He didn't have to take more then one guess as to who that one person would be. As he rounded the corner the voice matched his mental guess.

"So, my damn tea is served nearly cold, yeah know good tea has to be brought to a boil or you trying to pinch a few pennies and reuse them bags twice. And I'm still waiting for my cookies." It was Helen Lavoie, spitfire and Irish fury. She was in her late seventies. Roy smiled at her haphazardly cut hair she refused to let anyone else cut her hair. "No one's going near me with anything that sharp, liable to slice off one of my ears," she said once. Hair that was once gorgeous blonde, now thoroughly grayed by the touch of time. Roy had seen pictures of her when she was much younger, she had been a very good-looking woman in her day.

"Well good day Helen." There weren't too many here that retained their full mental capacities. Helen, unfortunately for the staff, was one. "The devil, that hot-tempered son of a bitch, will take me in his care someday, but there's going to be a lot of kicking and screaming on the way down," she had told him one day. That was something, Roy had no doubt about in his mind whatsoever. Roy had many a lively conversation with Helen every time he came to visit his son. Helen was dressed in a dark blue dress, emblazoned with bright red flowers, probably the brightest and most alive individual in this hospital, including the staff, he pondered. Roy had repeatedly tried to get Mrs. Leighton into this care facility, he knew Helen and her would become best friends. They were like twins, both feisty and spirited. Friends for each other instead of two lonely women apart. Mrs. Leighton had steadfastly refused.

Helen turned around and gave Roy a big smile, walked up to him and planted a kiss on his cheek as she wrapped her arms around him. "If it isn't the best-looking man I've seen in this dive since your last visit. Excuse me a moment I've a little unfinished business to attend to." Helen pushed Roy aside with a strength that was surprising for someone of her age. Roy stood there with his hands crossed in front of him, he knew better than to interfere when Helen was on a determined warpath.

Helen strode up to the desk, where a young girl, either Spanish or Filipino, sat. The girl looked quite young and innocent. "I already said I can't get any cookies from the kitchen, for you."

Helen deftly pulled off one of her red shoes and waved it into the air. "Either get me some cookies for my tea or this computer screen will be wearing a new ornament."

"Okay, okay, relax Miss Lavoie, I'll see what I can get from the kitchen."

Mollified, Helen turned around and winked at Roy. "If this were a damn hotel I'd check out at midnight and leave them holding the bag."

Roy smiled, he hoped when he got her age he'd retain half the spark that she did. Perhaps it was the zest in her that appealed to him in all the women that he seemed to attract into his life. Julia-Rae wasn't any different, inside her dwelt such a fire. The way she had nearly attacked him on that hiking trail and not to mention the scene at the door to her hotel room last night. The electricity between them was incredible. If he'd stayed another second longer Julia-Rae would have attacked him in that hallway. But he wanted her alone, on his grounds and with time to think about him. Roy smiled, maybe Antonio was right, when he said stay away from that one, she's trouble. Was he actually teasing her, or himself? Or was it just the fear that he'd started something that was way over his head and like jumping into a raging white-water whirlpool. Knowing in hindsight it was too late to pull back out.

Roy made a mental note to bring a box of cookies for Helen on his next visit.

"Come on handsome, can you imagine serving tea and no cookies to dip into it. What a revolting establishment.

Let's go visit that son of yours. I imagine you haven't much time."

"Right again, Helen." Roy fell into step with her, feeling just a little guilty about her last comment. It was true he often only stayed for an hour or so each visit. But he tried to see him as often as his busy schedule allowed.

"Well at least you come and visit, some of us only get the occasional visit during the obligated holidays, Christmas, Easter, birthdays, etc. You've been here nearly every week for the past few years." Helen turned on her heels, "and dearie, bring my tea outside, thanks." She said to the nursing attendant who scowled at her.

Roy smirked, after all of these years she still retained some semblance of her former beauty. He wondered what kind of fire this woman had when she was younger. They opened the doors and walked out into the manicured gardens of the nursing home. "So did Mr. Thurston drop by since I last saw you?"

Helen laughed a deep, lusty laugh. "You mean Mr. Typical Englishman Done-In-Two-Minutes-Flat Thurston," she snickered. "Darn English, no wonder they ruled the world once, anyone that quick on the draw has nothing but time left over to conquer the world."

Her laughter sounded incredibly good to Roy. There was something soothing about a woman's laughter. Especially when it comes deep and rich from the soul. Julia-Rae's laugh was like that.

"We met one steamy night in the gardens. Nothing like a little romance under a full moon surrounded by rose bushes," Helen sighed.

Roy didn't even want to imagine having sex at that age, although it was reassuring to know that one still could. "Let me guess it was over and done before you know it."

Helen sighed again, "Yah, you must have been there. Peeking through the rose bushes. But at least we're getting together again."

"How's my son doing lately?"

"He's doing fine, don't worry if they don't treat him proper, I'd up and let you know right away."

Roy had no doubt about that, he had left Helen his cellular phone number long ago just in case something ever came up. He was glad Helen was here to keep an eye on his son when he wasn't around.

Sean was sitting in his wheelchair staring up into the sky. Roy knew he was watching the clouds going by, a favorite past time of Sean's. Sean saw the two of them approaching and smiled, "sit, sit, daddy." He squealed in delight.

Roy sat down beside his twelve-year-old son. A sad smile crossed Roy's face. Sean sat with his tongue hanging out loosely from one corner of his mouth. One half of Sean's face sagged limply, as it had since the accident. Roy glanced down at the sheet of paper Sean had scrawled on. "What are you drawing?"

Sean pointed to the paper filled with crayoned squiggles and line and stuttered, “flowers.”

Roy stared at the abstract drawing. To his son they were flowers, Roy saw only scribbles. “Wow, such pretty flowers, are they from the flower garden?”

“No, Mickey’s house.” Sean shook his head in disbelief, beside him lay a picture book of Mickey Mouse.

“Wow, Mickey grows some pretty nice flowers.”

“The pictures for you, daddy.”

Roy stared at his, son. Sean had the same slightly curly blonde hair, the set jaw and the same blue eyes as himself. Roy sagged a little, feeling small in his three-piece suit. The major difference was that Sean’s eyes no longer shone with any intelligence. That, Roy had taken away eight years ago.

The nursing attendant brought by the tea and cookies for Helen. Helen remained quiet as Roy and Sean chatted, probably not wanting to take away from Roy’s attention to

Sean. Roy was always thankful for that whenever he came over to visit.

In the background Roy heard someone else ask for more tea. “I haven’t had enough to drink yet,” they said.

“I haven’t had enough to drink yet.” A weariness, born of old memories buried deep within but not forgotten, seeped into his soul. How many times in the past had he expressed those very words?

The same words he’d last uttered once before at a friend’s place, nearly nine years ago during a surprise birthday party for himself came flooding back.

Roy chugged back another vodka and seven.

Carrie looked worried. “I think I’ll drive Roy.”

“Don’t be silly, I’ve only had a few, I’ll be fine.”

“Roy you always say that, the last time you were nearly falling down drunk.”

“I was not, I merely had to tie my shoelaces and tripped,” he bent over and tried to tie his shoes laces as the world began to move in disconcerting circles. Unable to tie the laces Roy then tucked them in the sides of his shoes. “There done.”

“I’ll put Sean in the back seat, he’s already asleep,” Carrie said.

Roy turned to his friend, Ivan, hovering at the kitchen table. “And I believe I’ll have another one for the road,” he laughed.

“She’s pretty upset,” Ivan sputtered, his booze laden breath assailed Roy’s nose. It was a good thing that Ivan was at home he had a lot more to drink then Roy did. “I’ll get your coat,” he said and staggered down the hall.

“Yah, she thinks I drink too much.” Roy sat down by the table.

“You do!” Carrie said, her voice rising. Carrie had Sean slumped over in his arms as she stomped out the door.

“Well, if I’m going to get yelled at I better make it worthwhile,” he laughed as Ivan returned with his coat. Roy poured himself another drink.

Roy vividly remembered the yelling in the car after, the rain hammering on a windshield that he could barely see out of on a clear night, let alone in his present shape and he especially remembered the lights.

The lights of the oncoming truck.

He must have swerved over the white line of the road as he was trying to wipe the condensation collecting on the inside of the windshield. A desperate honk, bright lights, the crunch of metal and the tinkle of shattering glass. Then a blank emptiness.

Jagged, splintered flashes were all he had of his next few months. Just snapshot images as he struggled to remain alive. Hospital. Morphine. Pain, intense pain, with every breath he took. Visitors. Pain. Stitches. A body, his broken, beyond belief. Pain. Someone, a visitor, his mother? Telling him details of Carrie's funeral, a funeral he'd never be able to attend now. All he could do was visit the headstone many months later and cry. A doctor relating details of his son's condition; massive head contusions from being flung through the windshield. Sean would never walk again; his spinal cord was badly damaged and he'd be mentally retarded for the rest of his life. More pain as he tried to walk again. It didn't stop for a long time. Some of the pain, he knew, still lingered and probably would for the rest of his life. The pain in his heart, the ache in his soul. An emptiness deep inside, that he feared would always remain locked around his heart. An emptiness that Julia-Rae threatened to rip asunder. Would he be able to take the pain, especially after she found out what he was up to? That was the last time Roy had touched a drop of alcohol. He committed that to the darkness of his past, along with Carrie's memory.

Roy blinked and focused on the face of his son sitting in the wheelchair before him. He knew the physical pain had stopped long ago. The mental anguish would never stop, somehow he just got used to feeling it. A numbness that crept into his heart and kept it frozen. Unfeeling, un-hurting. What if he couldn't love again? Or was he prepared to take that risk with Julia-Rae? She was a woman that could arouse the deepest passions in any man and in him. Was he ready to go there? Could he take the chance and try to take over her business and keep his heart from falling in love? Or was it too late?

Roy slumped slightly, who was he trying to kid, when she found out what she was up to, and she would someday, she'd probably throw him out on the street.

Roy walked out into the parking lot and sat in his car. His hands gripped the steering wheel, knuckles whitening. He stared at the reflection in the mirror. "It never gets any easier, does it?" Tears puddled in the corners of his eyes but never fell. He had cried enough tears long ago. Life had to go on.

A flood, another virtual flood of mail sat on Julia-Rae's desk. With a sigh she sat down and began the long and boring process of sorting through it all. Well, bungie jumping had been a success in more ways than one, not to mention him showing up at Lake Louise. It never occurred to her until now to ask, how he knew she would be at the same time?

That man was too good to be true, she had agreed to meet him Saturday night at his condo. Shivers still ran down her spine recalling the pleasure of staring into his eyes. His firmness, the comfort of his arms as they were tied together. What was it about him and those eyes that drew her in? She could stare at those eyes all day. Perhaps the rest of her life. Nah, that was crazy.

Cindy knocked on Julia-Rae's door and entered the office. "So how was the media bungee jump?" She asked.

"Incredible, what a rush, you should try it someday."

"No thank you, I'll not be willing jumping off a two-hundred-foot platform with only an elastic band tied around my ankles and call it fun." Cindy shuddered. "I've got everything together for the next issue. The articles have been typed up. The expose on Hong Kong looks good. But I noticed something odd about the pictures."

"Oh, what is that?"

"Well, I'm not quite sure how to say this but those pictures are from the same set of pictures as these I spotted in an issue of Intrepid magazine. Which, as you know is put out by the Stanza group.

"What are you talking about?"

"Well take a look at this." Cindy brought a copy of Intrepid magazine out of the stack of papers in her arms and placed it before Julia-Rae.

She glanced at the cover date. "How could you possibly have spotted something like that in a year old copy of our competition's magazine?"

"It is my job to keep abreast of the competition and keep us one step ahead of them, one does that by keeping in touch with everything they have done and what they're going to be doing."

As Julia-Rae flipped open the magazine she made a mental note to give this girl a raise first chance she got. She stopped at the spread on Hong Kong. Cindy placed copies of the pictures beside the magazine.

"They're virtually the same pictures, check out the flowers."

Julia-Rae looked closely at the group of brilliant yellow and red roses. "So what, anyone can take a picture at the same location as these."

"Look closer."

There on both pictures, crawling around the two same roses were two wasps. There was no doubt that the pictures were shot by the same person at almost the same time.

“You’re right. Did he enclose a release to allow us the use of the pictures?”

“As a matter of fact, he did.”

Julia-Rae turned and walked up to her filing cabinet. She flipped through it until she found the file she wanted. On a handwritten note was scrawled “These pictures are for your pleasure to use as you desire. PS, I’m also at your disposal for the same.” A shiver ran through Julia-Rae as she read those words. The idea of him waiting for her, to use at her pleasure as she desired, sent a jolt of heat through Julia-Rae. He sure knew how to incite her desires. She flashed back to him pressed up behind her at the door to her hotel room at Lake Louise. His closeness, the heat of his body, and the erotic sensations of his breath caressing the back of her neck. She shook her head, this was work, Julia-Rae, not Fantasy Island.

"Well, I did go ahead and also phone Intrepid magazine and ask who the photog on the article was. All they would willing pass on to me was the initials RS."

"Nothing else?"

"No, they won't divulge any information about anyone in any of their articles."

"That's odd, he didn't say anything to me about being published with anyone in regards to these particular pictures. But then again, I really didn't ask."

"Well, we've got your note, so legally we're ok."

"Okay so we proceed with the articles, have those pictures scanned and take out the wasps, just in case someone else notices the similarity in the pictures."

"Done, with the digital scanner it won't take long to do and we'll have the article ready to roll for our next issue by tonight."

"Good." Julia-Rae stared at the pictures. Why hadn't Roy mentioned that they were recently published? Especially with the organization that was in the process of trying to buy her out. Then again maybe he didn't know. She made a mental note to ask him tomorrow when they got together. Just her alone with him, on his territory. An electric jolt of desire rippled across her. He was definitely the type to try something and she was definitely willing to be experimented on.

Julia-Rae opened the file she had asked him to send her of the pictures he took when they were on Machu Picchu. She had nearly forgotten about those pictures, the ones of the plateau light up below them when they stood on the platform. Some of those she might be able to use. From the file a single picture stood out of herself. It was the one he had taken of her with her hair being caressed by the high mountain wind. The redness of her cheeks and the spark of living on the edge radiated from her face. Roy had slipped it amongst the pictures he had sent her. The pictures had a freshness, an aliveness to it that seemed to be lacking in the ones she had taken. It spoke to her, called her with a stunningly allure of a woman of today. The free spirit, the passion, sensitivity and commitment that she tried so hard to instill into everything Julia-Rae strived to put into her magazine. It was all there in this one picture. The man definitely had the gift of capturing spirit on film.

Chapter Eight

Roy sat beside the window in Mrs. Leighton's apartment. She had insisted on bringing tea to him. "Can I get those for you?" He said feeling guilty for letting her serve him.

"Nonsense, if I wanted you to bring the tea out I'd have asked, now sit and relax."

He did, he knew she liked doing stuff like bringing him tea, it made her feel useful, Roy thought, she didn't have much else she could do in her life.

"Now," she said setting the silver tray with Earl Grey tea, two English bone China cups and saucers and a plate of rich shortbread cookies.

"You really should stop eating food this rich Mrs. Leighton." He'd long ago asked if she liked that more than being called by her first name, Angie. It somehow seemed more respectful.

"Hey at my age what's one day more? I've lived this long and I ain't stopping now." She sat down with a heavy thud, obviously tired. "Now where did we leave off?"

Roy picked up a copy of Hot Colorado Weekend, "chapter two, I believe."

"Oh yeah, she's going up to his room to bring him the bubble bath. I think he'll be doing more to her than lathering soap. I know he's already got her in a lather."

Roy shook his head, she'd never change. Same crazy lady he had loved all these years. She had so much of Carrie in her, Roy frowned for a moment. Speaking of crazy ladies and working up a lather Julia-Rae came to his mind. He was having a hard time keeping that fiery red head out of his mind. What wild insidious temper. What wild passions lay inside that one? He couldn't wait to unearth Saturday night. The sensations of having her tied up against him, her breasts crushing his. Her nipples growing hard with excitement. Her mouth parting wanting him to kiss her, just before they went over the edge of the Bungie jump. If they a few more seconds they'd have been kissing. Just like when he had her pinned up against the door to her hotel room or better yet in the mountain hike at Lake Louise. She had nearly ripped his clothes off. Yes, he had her right where he wanted her, now he had to begin going in for the kill. But not before a little pleasure, like tomorrow night promised to bring. Pleasure and perhaps a lot of regret. Don't get emotionally attached, he thought. Too frigging late.

"Hey Mister Lost In Some World Beyond The Twilight Zone."

"Oh sorry, I was a thinking of-"

"Of some hot lady you met, I bet."

"Well, now that you mention it."

"I knew it, you got the same wanderlust look that last hero had in that last romance book you read me. So, tell me her name." As if she read his mind.

Roy hesitated, it was harder then he thought, telling Mrs. Leighton about another woman. Somehow it didn't seem right, out of consideration for her daughter.

"Hey, it's okay, Carrie passed away and you have to get on with life. I'd be thrilled if you told me about this new lady."

"Really?" Roy sat quiet for a moment. "She's Julia-Rae McNaughton and runs one of competitors magazines. I met her one day while doing some pictures for an article on Machu Picchu." Mrs. Leighton sat quiet and very attentive.

"She has wild flowing red hair and wild disposition to match." "Oh yeah, how wild," she asked excitedly.

When we met, I accidentally broke her camera lens and later she stormed up behind me and thwapped me in the rear with her bandanna."

“Haa-a, a woman with spirit and fire. God, I love it, ha!” Angie roared until she began coughing.

Roy was amazed how she could cough so hard and not spit up body parts. Roy sat quiet as Mrs. Leighton calmed down and finally sipped on her tea.

She set down her teacup, “well it’s about damn time. Look, I never told you and we never really talked about her death. I was pissed at the time and wanted to tear your face off. Now, like you I just miss her and life has to go on for the living.”

Roy sat quiet. He couldn’t really tell Angie that this crazy, mad impetuous woman he had met with the intention of seducing and taking over her company. Maybe Antonio was right. Maybe he had better be careful and stick to the original plan. Seduce her, take her mind off the takeover. It sounded easy enough at first. Easy until he began to get to know her. One of the things Roy realized was her reasons for running her own business, the pride of ownership and being in control were exactly the same reasons he ran his business. Taking that away from Julia-Rae McNaughton he knew would rip her heart out, as it would his if that happened to him.

"Hey knock it off with the Mr. Quiet routine, you sure have a funny way of showing your head over heels in love."

"In love? I'm not. . ." Was he? The words hit a little hard, could it be possible? Had she begun to walk down corridors of his heart he swore he'd never let anyone ever walk again? Damn maybe Antonio had seen something all along.

"Okay, tell you what let's skip the gaiety and laughter and read me that novel."

"Sure, sounds good." He turned open the paperback. Julia-Rae's face swam before him. All he could think about was those parted lips, waiting, wanting his against hers. Damn, he was in trouble. Roy wondered who really had who right were they wanted them?

In Julia-Rae's office a message blinked on her Email screen. It was a private message on her Facebook page, from Roy.

>Contact me regarding Cross Dressing Media Party at Hilton

6:00 Friday RS<

>HI are you online now?< She could see that he was.

>Yes, as a matter of fact I am, interested? Or should I say have you got the guts to dress like a man?<

>Whoa, them's fighting words pardner. I'll wear anything a man can wear. Can you wear anything a woman can?<

>Darn right. Meet me at Tiffany's masquerade downtown Friday 4:00. You pick an outfit and I've got one in mind for you, no chickening out.<

>Bets on and no crying, I hate bawl babies.<

Julia-Rae giggled she knew exactly what she wanted him to wear. She'd see what mettle this man really possessed.

"Hello." The signal lights on Jasper Avenue had just turned red and Roy was stuck in the lineup with his car. Roy glanced around unable to get to the side of the road. He never tested but decided to take the call on his cell while he waited in line. There were only two people in the world that knew this phone number.

"Well, it's good to hear from you, how did the escapade in Banff work?"

It was Antonio. "Quite well, I'm on my way to meet her for that Crossdressing Media Party and then we're meeting tomorrow night at my place for dinner and who knows what after."

"Good, look I've just gone over the books before the stockholders meeting next week Friday and it looks worse then I thought. We need to move and move fast Roy, I've a couple of ideas."

The light turned green and Roy began to accelerate easy on the throttle of his restored 1997 black Toyota Supra, he knew its twin turbocharged engine had way too much power for the icy roads that were sure to be soon happening in Edmonton's infernally long, cold winters. But then he always had his Ford Expedition to rely on. "What's up your sleeve?"

"Well, I'm prepared to up our offer and if she refuses, like I think she will, then I'll make a buyout offer to her secretary. Like you mentioned, she's the linchpin that could set this whole business into play. I took Cindy for lunch one day after we talked and I'm pretty sure she'd leave if we upped her salary enough. That would leave Julia-Rae in a fine mess."

Roy slowed down a block later, too bad these lights weren't better coordinated, he thought. Now wishing he hadn't told Antonio about Cindy. "That seems a little harsh."

"Harsh? I think perhaps you are getting a little soft, my friend. Where is the killer instinct Ray Sutfield that I know? That woman is getting to you, I know amour in a man's eyes when I see it."

"Okay I get your point, perhaps you're right. Also in that new offer put the condition that she will remain in control as the president, one of the issues for her is not money, but the pride of running her own show." The second light turned green and Roy eased forward again. He didn't want to hurt Julia-Rae anymore than was needed. "Approach her Monday, after our rendezvous Saturday night, hopefully I'll have softened her up enough to make her change her mind."

"Okay, I'll do that, besides after we take over we can turf her out for some bogus reason. Ciao."

Roy clicked off the cellphone and concentrated on driving through the traffic. He hadn't realized until now just how ruthless Antonio was. What was that he had read someplace long ago about "He who rides on the back of the tiger often winds up inside." The bone white of razor sharp teeth and the arid, fetid breath of animal decay singed his senses. Where he was right now in his life he didn't know, but one thing Roy did know was that he didn't feel like he was riding on the back of this tiger anymore.

"Did I ever mention you had sexy legs?" Julia-Rae spat her wad of chewing tobacco in the spittoon and wiped the residue from her mustache. They were in the back of Walter's Masquerade shop, no one else was there to interrupt them. The taste of the tobacco was absolutely hideous, like a mouthful of tar. What men liked about chewing tobacco she couldn't ever understand, must be that male macho thing. She was dressed in a cowboy outfit, complete with chaps, ten-gallon hat and handlebar mustache. Roy had really gone all out to try and embarrass her. She had suffered the taste of the tobacco, knowing pay back time was about to arrive.

"And," Roy carefully pulled his pantyhose over the stubble of his legs in the adjacent dressing room, "did I ever call you one twisted puppy?"

There was no one in the back where they were changing.

"Wait a minute, are you backing out? Wasn't this Crossdressing party your idea?"

Roy rose and stared at his reflection of his legs in the mirror.

"Damn, I think I've got a run."

"Here let me see."

Julia-Rae glanced through the slight part in the doorway and caught a partial view of his backside. She started to giggle at the sight and leaned against the wall bursting into full-blown laughter. She tried stopping long enough to remove the rest of the wad of tobacco and nearly gagged in the process.

"What in the world are you laughing at," Roy muttered focused on the run and the eerie cool feeling of hose on his legs.

"Turn around," Julia-Rae tried staying composed, she wanted to look in the room but didn't have the guts. She only caught a partial view of him from the shoulders down as he turned.

Roy turned and stared into the mirror, "Damn."

Julia-Rae staggered back to her dressing room and collapsed into her chair. Tears rolled down her face.

"Very funny, Julia-Rae, very funny. You didn't tell me these were crotch-less!" He stared at his manhood meekly staring at the floor, shrinking in the unexpected cool air.

"Bahh-h," Julia-Rae bellowed not even trying to control herself any longer.

"I can't possibly wear this."

“What, afraid of - drafts?” She wiped at the tears streaking her face. This was too much. “I know what the deal was, I wear anything you might, normally wear and you wear anything I might normally wear.”

“Yeah, but,” Roy stopped for a moment as the realization sunk in. “You mean you would wear something like this?”

“Well ordinarily no; but ask me out on a hot date and you might find out someday, and you thought the mustache and chewing tobacco would stop me.”

Roy stared at his reflection. A lustful smile crept over his face. What would she look like wearing these? He had met this woman only a couple of weeks ago and she was every bit as nuts as he was, maybe more. He was certain she enjoyed his outlandish brand of humor also. He was supposed to be seducing her in order to buy out her company. He wondered who was seducing whom, Antonio was right.

He had better be careful, only was it too late? “Okay I’ll wear the dress, but no makeup.”

“Not even a little rouge and lipstick? What kind of a cross-dresser are you?”

“One that suddenly appreciates jockey shorts, tee-shirts, a cold beer and a clean shave. Okay, I agreed to this, I better go all the way, besides if I’ve makeup on maybe no one will recognize me.”

“Good point, I just happen to have brought my makeup bag along.” Julia-Rae laughed.

“Oh great, and I thought this whole thing was my idea.”

“It was, it was,” she reassured him, “I just happen to think fast on my feet.” This party was going to be a good test, to see how well they’d do in public. Together, as a couple? That thought so foreign to her, came naturally. Julia-Rae liked the sound of it, a couple.

Chapter Nine

Julia-Rae stood on the edge of Roy's balcony, below the lazy North Saskatchewan river flowed by. His condo was in the expensive Le Marchand Tower that stood on the high banks of the river. It commanded a spectacular view. The condo wrapped in a gorgeous semi-circle around the building, in fact each floor had only three suites. The balcony alone had more space than the backyard she grew up in as a child.

The heavily wooded North Saskatchewan River valley, a rarity in large cities and highly treasured by Edmontonians, wound its way around a large bend. It circled the river like a lover's pair of thighs would, wrapping itself around the shimmering water. Moonlight stole across the water; it was one of those still late summer nights on the prairies. One of those soulless evenings, warm but not too hot, just right for nights of passion.

The door to the balcony swished open, her and Roy were alone. The evening had been wonderful. Roy had cooked a fabulous meal, another thing about him that had surprised her, he didn't look like the gourmet dinner kind of guy. But he had mentioned that he had been a bachelor for quite awhile. There were many things about Roy that Julia-Rae found pleasantly surprising. This man in the crazy Peruvian smock, had exuded nothing but sensuality all night. From the candlelight dinner, with Mozart playing in the background, to the gas fireplace surrounded by candles. Yes, he was a pleasant surprise this Roy Sutter.

"Enjoying the view," he casually remarked as he handed her a chilled glass of white wine.

Chardonnay the wine of lovers, or soon to be Julia-Rae hoped. A tingle ran through her, perhaps she had a glass too many already. "Yes, I was." Her fingers touched his as she reached for the glass. A delicious thrill ran through her. Why did it seem like everything about him excited her? Everything from his merest smile to just the look in his eyes as he stared at her.

“I don’t often enjoy this view,” he shared. “During the winter I’m usually out somewhere on the road, or at least that’s how I try to arrange it. It gets pretty cold here.”

Julia-Rae noted the sadness in his voice. “Well, I’m sure you’ve had many a young lady over to share those lonely cold nights, when you’ve been here.”

“You’re the first woman I’ve had here in the last couple of years.”

“Oh, why is that? Surely you aren’t embarrassed to show this place off.”

Roy didn’t want to tell her about his past, about Carrie, his drinking and his son. No, he never wanted to bring up that part of his past to anyone. Let alone her. He sipped at his glass of dealcoholized wine, craving it was the real thing. "Just too much focus on work, I guess."

Something in the inflection of his voice told Julia-Rae that there was much more to Roy then work. But this wasn't the time or place to get into it. "Thanks for the wonderful meal," she said trying to shift the conversation. "Thanks also for taking me out to the Cross-Dressing party yesterday, it was a blast." They had smoozed with some interesting folks, some of which she wasn't sure if they were really men dressed as women or vice versa. But one thing she did know about the transgender crowd, they were an interesting and electric group of people. She had kept pretty close to Roy the whole night, more out of security than anything else. Now that she thought about it, it did feel pretty good having him there as support. Something she wasn't at all used to in her life. She always had to go it alone, trusting her own instincts. Relying on no one but herself to get her through life and that in itself could be a very liberating feeling. Liberating to be in control of one's own destiny and create it as she desired, that and lonely.

"It was, wasn't it? I enjoy doing things that can benefit others."

"Yes, so do I, we raised quite a bit of money last night." Was that her voice growing huskier or just the wine? Roy walked around her. Perhaps he was just trying to get a better view. All Julia-Rae knew was his nearness sent a shiver through her. There wasn't much about this enigmatic man that didn't thrill her. How could he arouse in her this kind of passion?

He stared out enjoying the view of the river valley. Julia-Rae caught the reflection of his hair in the moonlight. He reminded of some golden angel, the way the light danced off his hair casting it in a golden hue. What moved inside this enigmatic man? What was he thinking? Nothing about him made any sense, nothing about him was stale. He was like a fresh breeze blowing in off the coast. Clean, unexplored, unknown. Something about that excited her. Something about being here, alone in his place, excited her. Dinner was over and she was sure he would try something with her. Actually she wanted him to try something. "I've had a wonderful evening, you surprise me."

"In what way?"

"Well, you didn't strike me as a man that can cook a fabulous meal and don't get me wrong the meal was absolutely gorgeous."

"Ah, then I must strike you as the rotten ronnie type then."

"No, well yes, I've got to admit when I first saw you scrambling on those rocks in Machu Picchu, dressed in a smock and tattered jeans.

. ."

"Unshaven and unkempt."

"You looked very," savage, almost primal, she wanted to say. Julia-Rae had never seen a man skirt over sheer rock cliffs that would make a mountain lion think twice, while dangling assorted camera equipment from his neck. "Much like you belonged on that cliff."

Roy moved closer to her. He caught hints of gardenia on the gentle breeze that blew. Her perfume reminded him of the flower, he wanted to run his face through her hair and luxuriate in the fragrances he smelt coming from her. Even in the moonlight her red hair seemed to be on fire. Not unlike the fires that were being stirred in him. What would it be like to have her in his arms? Moaning with desire, desire for him. The hot course of blood, pounding through his loins sent a quiver through him. All he had set out to do was seduce her and buy out her business. Simple enough. Seduce a beautiful woman and buy out her business, easy.

It was easy until he got to the getting to know her part. She was wild, impetuous and crazy, so much like him. That fiery bundle fire didn't reflect her nature, it was more like it tried to contain the energy and fury that blazed within her. Energy that threatened to set her on fire and him also. He had already tasted her lips he knew what touching her would do to him and to her. She had come so passionately alive when they had kissed. When she had pushed him back against that blanket on the mountainside. Something about that kind of aggression, of her wanting to be in control, on top like an awakening tigress. That excited him in ways he didn't quite understand yet, so much like Carrie had been.

Somewhere inside Roy felt something fall, like the petals falling off a rose, a dried out old rose of Carrie' memory. A memory slowly being pushed out of the way by new growth, by Julia-Rae. Was he really ready for this? What was he saying, all he had to do was seduce her and talk her into selling the business. That was the goal, stick to it like Antonio said. So what was tugging at him? What was it about her that threatened to open old wounds and allow him to look at something and feel something he had denied himself to feel in a long time? He had to get out of this line of thought and fast. “Sometimes when I’m taking pictures it’s like everything around me becomes nonexistent. I am merely an observer. I focus on what I want and the object I want photographed. Often, I’m moving to the flow of my focus, it tells me how it wants to be pictured and I am merely just the camera.”

He turned to look at Julia-Rae and realized she was standing right beside him. Her eyes were a sensuous smoky whirling mist.

“I know exactly what you mean. In a way it’s like becoming part of the picture and speaking of cameras thank you for the Hong Kong pictures.”

“Did they help you?”

“Yes, I used three for my article, I can’t say thank you enough. Although you could have told me some were published in my competition magazine, Intrepid.”

“Intrepid?” Roy hesitated for a moment; he hadn’t expected her to find out the pictures were actually published once before. “Interesting, I just give the prints to my agent and I’ve no idea where they go from there. Besides, you don’t need to say thank you, just the smile in your eyes is reward enough.”

“Oh, come on now, there must be some way I can repay you.”

“Well, my usual price is five hundred per picture, but in your case I’d settle for a single kiss per picture.” Roy turned and stared into her smoldering eyes.

“A very steep price indeed sir, how will I ever live up to the fare imposed upon my fair heart.” Julia-Rae spoke in a falsetto voice, mimicking a damsel in distress. “I am eternally indebted to your kindness and immense generosity good sire.”

“Then you must kiss me once and thrice and be forever beholden to me fair maiden.” Roy remembered the words from one of the books he had recently read Mrs. Leighton.

Julia-Rae stepped closer. "I do not know if I can besmirch my honor." She stepped closer until they were touching, the heat from his body set little tingles of hunger through her like brush fires singeing across her skin.

His eyes glistened with the hunger of a lone wolf perched on the edge of a forest's mists. Threatening, blending into the shrouds of vapor, but there, with a determined hunger. The wolf with an insatiable appetite and she shuddered realizing the only thing that would sate that hunger was her.

"Not as much as I want to besmirch you." Roy put his arms around Julia-Rae and pulled her to him. Her fragrance was intoxicating, of soft wine and gentle flowers. He reached up and brushed one hand across her face moving a windswept strand of misbehaving red hair out of the way. Every tingling nerve, every maddening pump of his heart cried out to have her now. He crushed his lips to hers as he held her face with his one hand. Afraid to let go, in case this vision of hunger and passion should evaporate like the mists of the mountain valleys in the morning.

Softly at first their lips crushed together, his tongue darted out to flick across her lips, as if to taste some delicate morsel. Julia-Rae moaned. As her own tongue flickered against his and drew his into her mouth and she crushed her lips to his with a hunger that had been too long denied.

Roy pulled away after seconds that seemed like an eternity of passion. “Let’s sit down by the fire its warmer there.”

“Yes, I’m getting a bit chilly.”

Julia-Rae moved with the ease that mists float through still mountain valleys, her heart pounding and a hunger tore straight to the place that she desired to have him. She was surprised he didn’t see her legs shaking. She sank into the reassuring softness of the couch, one of those soft enveloping type of couches that nestled gently around you. “I love the couch, it's my style, soft and luxurious." The weight of his body sinking next to her drew her to him.

"Do you now?" The gas fireplace flickered in the background. "I would sooner prefer the smell of real wood smoke, one of my favorite things about camping. But at least this is convenient, not to mention romantic."

"I love campfires, used to go on those with my dad when I was younger all the time."

"Were you close to your dad, then?"

"Yeah, my mom died after I was born and dad raised me like his little boy that he always wanted."

"Sorry to hear that. I guess I was blessed with regular parents, I was the oldest of three."

Roy looked into Julia-Rae's eyes as he sat beside her. Words, just words, slipped away on the air stirred by the warmth of the fires flickers and stirred by the fires that burned.

Roy studied her face as she talked and finally raised his arm and lightly pressed his middle finger to her lips. He slid in beside her. The silent flickering of the fireplace was all that broke the suddenness stillness. Roy pulled his finger away and slowly brought his lips against hers. To let another moment go by, without kissing those soft, red lips, was unbearable. He wanted to feel her lips against him again. He wanted, no hungered, to experience that passion, that fire that they had begun on the mountainside. A sweet gasp escaped her lips as he placed his lips on hers. To kiss her slowly, deliciously and savor this moment.

Julia-Rae's lips tasted of sweet wine, softness and promise, sweet tender promise. The jasmine of her perfume flooded his nose, begging him to act on his compulsions. Roy pulled Julia-Rae into his arms and at first, gently kissed her. The softness of her lips like the crush of satiny silk aroused him. His lips were on fire, hers were the fuel feeding them.

Their lips parted and Roy slid his tongue into Julia-Rae's wanting mouth. Their tongues danced together in an erotic, arousing movement.

Roy pulled back for a moment, never had a woman's kiss aroused the fires of his soul like she did. Julia-Rae opened her eyes for a moment, brought out from her world of pulsing hungry desires.

In that flicker of her soul's eye Roy saw what he had been denying himself for far too long. To continue this he knew now would lead to far more then just a one time fling. To kiss her again would be to draw his soul into orbit with a far greater power then he could ever possess the strength to break free. The glint inside her eye told him that she instinctively knew this also. That her soul had already, deny it or not, begun to settle into the world of his spinning. Falling ever deeper into the gravity of his being.

Roy darted his tongue along her lips, teasing her. Julia-Rac moaned. He licked at the base of her throat, running his tongue up to her ear and with a hungry hot breath, breathed into her ear, “I want you.” It was that plain and simple. Every muscle in his body began to sing of the desire to be in her, united with her. Driving herself and him wild with the basest of passions.

“Take me to your bedroom,” Julia-Rae gasped in return.

“Are you sure?” He knew she was sure, he just wanted to hear her confirmation of the hunger she felt for him. He wanted to say something inept and funny like we’re not on a trail with other hikers to interrupt us but didn’t. This wasn’t a time for saying something silly.

“Yes Roy, I want you, need you.”

“Come with me,” he said as he stood up and took her hand in his. His voice deep and husky with hunger. The hiss of the fire dwindled into the background as he led her to his bedroom.

Roy lit a candle; it pulled the darkness of the room back into the corners. Everywhere on the walls pictures flickered into view, brought to life by the soft light of the candle. Photographs adorned the walls in a haphazard array like ancient pictographs scattered over dimly lit cavern walls by a prehistoric Rembrandt.

They were incredible, Julia-Rae stared, drawn into the pictures Roy had taken over the years.

One of a picture on a beach, or so it looked like a beach, but it was hard to tell. The clean sand melded into the flow of the ocean so serenely it was as if they were one with no definable edge. Cast in the center lay a resting eagle on a log, its face softened by the glow of the dawn's light. It looked so at ease, almost contemplating, as if it questioned its own savage existence or was asking the sea for forgiveness from the carnivorous nature of its soul.

Another of the crumbling remains of a totem pole. The bleached remains alone in a crowd of living green, vibrant trees. Cousin cedars to the totem, that stood alone, a reminder of a past that no longer existed. On the top corner of the totem a marten perched looking down at a face on the totem. Almost as if it was wondering who or what this was. This fading grotesque native God carved from the wood and slowly being reabsorbed.

A third picture was of a woman, a gorgeous blond dressed in hikers shorts perched on an outcropping of rock that jutted away from the edge of the mountain. All around her only empty air and mist curling up from the valleys thousands of feet below. Yet she was not afraid, instead she wore a satisfied look, a look of achievement, of pride. If there was ever a picture that Julia-Rae could use to represent her magazine that would be the one. It spoke of everything she believed and everything she wanted to instill in the women that read her magazine.

The pictures filled his walls, on and on, each one artwork to treasure. Tugging at her heart, her sensitivity.

Where did he get the soul to capture such gentle, and serene pictures?

Julia-Rae stood in awe, admiring the work of another not with the admiration of a student gazing at a master's work, not fully comprehending the entire scope depth and sheer magnificence, but with the appreciation of one that truly understood what it took to get the angles of the shots he took. The knowledge of the patience and care that had gone into each and everyone. "All of these yours, aren't they?" She knew they were, still she wanted to hear his voice and reassurance. Some of the places pictured she had been to before, others were a mystery. Later when it was appropriate she wanted to ask him so many questions.

"Yes," his voice called out hauntingly from the dimness of the room, "Yes, some of my personal favorites from over the years."

One picture in particular drew her in, it was of a little baby boy, she assumed, wrapped up in a blue towel, face still dripping fresh from a bath. Its face so familiar, stared out at her, she had seen that face somewhere else. It looked so tiny, so vulnerable and at the same time so full of new life and sparkle that rang in those little eyes. He had managed to capture the awe and wonder, innocence and the sparkle of emerging intelligence, that child possessed and that, perhaps every child, had.

Chapter Ten

His hands ran down her sides and into her hair as he kissed at the nape of her neck.

"I'd love to hear the stories behind these pictures."

"Sure, but right now there's something more important I'd rather be doing."

"Oh, what is that?"

"Making love to you," Roy whispered. The nearness of his body sent a current of electricity through her. He was standing just behind her; the shadow of his body threw itself up against the wall. Hers was lost in the darkness cast, like she wanted to be lost in the darkness of his soul.

Julia-Rae wanted to fall into his arms as she knew she was already falling into him and had been since she had met him. His hands, strong and sure, slowly unbuttoned her blouse. The same hands that had taken those pictures of such incredible sensitivity, now slide away her silk blouse and unclasped the hook of her bra. Neither spoke, only his ragged breathing and hers broke the silence. His hands sent tingles of arousal across the surface of her skin and left burning brushfires of hunger behind. Fires that now threatened to rage out of control, never had anyone managed to raise the kind of passion and hunger that he did. Too long had she bottled up her passion, Julia-Rae needed to release all the desires and hungers she had for this man. This incredible man.

Roy pulled at the straps of her black lace bra. The nearly inaudible swish of her bra sliding down to the ground reminded him of the slight swish of the Pacific breezes that stirred the palm trees of Maui. Each and everyone getting stronger, reminding the islanders that a storm was approaching. A storm was brewing and had been ever since he had nearly knocked over Julia-Rae on that mountain trail.

The softness of her skin called to him, the orchid fragrances wrapped themselves around him and drew him down to her. She was so delicate, so soft so irresistible. As Roy reached around and cupped her breasts, he caught a glimpse of them reflected in the picture of his little boy, Sean, wrapped in swaddling clothes. This scene he had played out once before, in another bedroom years ago. Him and Carrie, touching in this way, arousing. Only there was one difference, one subtle difference. Carrie never drew the reactions like Julia-Rae did every time she drew near him. Never had she drawn open passages in his heart, tore at the solid sensibilities that anchored him to the foundations of his maleness, to everything it meant to be a man. The urge to want, to take her. She incited feelings he had so long denied himself, feelings perhaps denied his entire life even with Carrie.

Julia-Rae moaned as the heat of his hands encased her breasts, her nipples she knew were extended, aroused, wanting first his touch then the hot wet kiss of his mouth on them and then to kiss her lower, where she desired him the most. She melted against his body, cradling in the strength of his maleness. Roy moved in response to Julia-Rae. She put her hands behind her and felt the hardness of him, his desire for her. He was in control, he set the pace. His breath and the wet, hot lick of his tongue on her neck as he softly caressed her breasts. Each delicate hair on her breasts were stirred and drawn to full life. The more he fondled her the hotter her breasts grew until they were on fire for him. She was lost in the erotic sensations of his hands caressing her breasts, playing with the hard nipples and gently cupping them, gently kneading her breasts. Slowly, reluctantly his hands slid down her body and began to undo her skirt.

His breath mingled with the non-alcohol wine and the heady musk of his cologne swirled around her as he whispered in her ear, "turn around."

As the skirt settled to the ground with a swish like the sigh of a warm breeze across heated sand, Julia-Rae turned around. Her breasts brushed against his body. Her hands shook a little as she pulled the ends of his shirt from the confines of his pants and she began to undo the buttons of his shirt, slowly exposing the dark hairs of his chest.

Julia-Rae gasped at the dark wonderful mat of chest hairs that lay in the center of his chest and outlined the ridges of each well-defined pec. The dark trail leads straight down the center of his ridged stomach to disappear behind the tight constraints of his slacks. She pulled back the arms of his shirt and as it slid to join the growing pile on the floor Julia-Rae put her arms around this appealing man and drew herself to him with a kiss. The softness of her breasts and skin crushed against the hardness of him and the coarseness of the dark, mysterious mat of hair that adorned his body. The exposed tender tips of her breasts buried themselves in that dark mat of chest hair. The fine delicate hairs on her breasts crushing against the course hairs of his chest. Her nipples, already hard with excitement, felt raw and tender against the harshness of his body.

Roy drew her head back and kissed those lips, the lips that set his heart singing and his emotions unleashed. “I want you very much, JR.” The erotic sensation of her soft breasts burrowing into his chest was nearly too much.

“Make love to me here and now, Roy.”

With the softness of her body calling out to him, Roy lost all resistance. His will had become the will of some sensual spirit calling out for the both of them to unite and create a new spirit, a new entity called them.

He gently pushed her unto the bed and struggled to pull the clips of his pants off as Julia-Rae gently pulled her panties down. Naked, Julia-Rae lay back on the pillow of his bed. Roy watched her rub her legs together in sensual splendor. He knew, she was so excited she could barely contain herself.

Her eyes focused on the hardness throbbing from his body as he pulled free his shorts and flung them into the corner. Her eyes drank in the sight of his naked body and focused on his throbbing member. Julia-Rae smiled and said, "This is what I wanted to see yesterday at the costume rental store."

He didn't have to respond to know she definitely liked what she saw. She watched him as he opened the drawer beside the bed and pulled the small plastic wrapped container free.

"Can I help put it on?" The idea of touching his hardness, stroking it, sent a rush through her. Never had she desired to do anything so much. She wanted to hold him in her mouth.

"No, I'd rather you didn't, this time, the next perhaps. If you touch me right now I'm afraid I'll explode," he gasped.

"Then hurry, my dear," Julia-Rae gasped.

Those words of endearment, sent a shiver through Roy. It was the first time she ever said something as tender as that. Roy pulled the rubber free and slowly unrolled it over himself. At least he knew the coating would keep away some of the sensations of being inside of her. Otherwise he was sure he'd explode the second he was inside of her.

So intense was his desire for Julia-Rae, never had Roy ever been this hungry to make love to a woman, ever. Would there be another time, a later date when he could make love without the use of the rubber? A tinge of sadness struck at him, perhaps not, sadly echoed through his head. Sooner or later, she would find out. This was supposed to be business, strictly business. Roy hoped it would be later, much later. Tonight, he would enjoy this to every moment, every breath. As if this was his last night on Earth and it could very well have been.

He looked at Julia-Rae lying naked on his bed, waiting for him. The candlelight dancing seductively over the curves of her body, auburn highlights cast over his pillow. Parts of her body hidden in folds of darkness, caverns of mystery that he would relish exploring later. She was gorgeous, stunningly gorgeous. Slowly she lifted her hand.

"Come to me," she smiled, "I need you."

A pulse of madness ran shuddering its way through him. He needed her, wanted her like he never wanted anything in his life.

Roy wanted to delay this for as long as possible, to enjoy this moment to the fullest. He sat by the edge of the bed and leaned over. He caressed the inside of her thighs with the hot moisture of his tongue.

Julia-Rae gasped, "Oh don't I'll…"

It was too late. He wanted to see all of her, taste all of her, drink in the nectar of her hunger for him. More than anything he wanted to savor this moment like a connoisseur samples the finest wine. Roy parted her legs and ran his tongue first down one side of where the lines of her panties had left a white area. An area of unknown erotic territory, of unknown pleasures. Then he skimmed the surface on the other side of her moist mound. That moist bed of curls, dark, sweet curls called to him. The milky fragrance of her wetness incited his tongue as he softly began to lick her.

"Oh…" she moaned arching her back like a cat languorously stretches itself sunning under a warm window. "Roy stop, I'm going to explode any second…"

Her plead fell on deaf ears. "Then explode my dear, because I'm not about to stop." Tremors began to course through her.

Julia-Rae put her hands on the back of his head and drew him in. Her legs pressed his body between them, trapping Roy.

Imprisoning him, Julia-Rae cried out in pleasure as she exploded.

Her legs tightened until he thought she would nearly choke him and then went limp. Roy stopped. Julia-Rae lay there convulsing in spasms of sheer pleasure. Roy merely watched her for a moment, enjoying the sensation of satisfying her as he kissed her wet warmth.

Her eyes opened, "thank you," she gasped "I've never experienced that before."

"You mean a man performing…"

"No, the orgasm. I thought it was me. Up until now I never truly enjoyed it long enough to allow myself the pleasure. That was incredible, thanks."

"It gets better." He smiled.

"How much?"

He rose and pulled himself up until he was on top of her. Looking into those moist eyes. Eyes that while looking satisfied, seemed to sparkle with new awaiting pleasures. "Let me show you, beautiful lady." Roy kissed those hot lips and parted them with the hunger of his tongue. He knew she could taste herself on him. That fierce passion awoke again as Roy entered her wetness with his manhood. He slowly inserted himself as she shuddered, still sensitive from her earlier explosions. Roy could feel the heat of her body all around him.

As Roy began to stroke himself inside of her Julia-Rae put her arms around him and dug her nails into her back. He'd have welts and claw marks there tomorrow, he didn't care. He was making love to this incredible woman with the re-awakening passions of a She-lion. Her legs drew, with an uncanny familiarity, over his. Each undulating thrust of their bodies brought a surge of pleasure singing through his loins. Roy was glad for the rubber otherwise he'd have exploded long before this. As it was, he could already feel the stirrings deep within.

Each stoke, calling to him, awakening his own need to explode. "I think - I'm going to…"

She pulled his head to hers. Her lips hungry to kiss his. Their tongues wrapped around each other. Julia-Rae cried out, "So am I, again."

The surge within like the ocean flooding through a rip tide channel swept through him and he knew through her. Roy felt her tightening and urging him on until he could spend no more.

Roy gasped and threw himself to the other side of the bed. Totally expended, he had nothing left to give her. He had given her everything he had inside. Everything except the open corridors of his heart and she was shaking the keys and rattling the chains. What would she do when she found out the truth? What would he do? Later, worry about it later, he just wanted to bathe in the sensations of this moment. Wanting it to last forever. This moment now was all that mattered in his soul.

Julia-Rae curled up beside him, in his arms. Each of them still convulsed in subsiding tremors, shaking in their delight. "That was easily the most satisfying moment of my life. You are incredible."

"As are you, as are you."

Julia-Rae wanted to say she loved him, yet the words stuck to her throat with the tenacity of a cornered wolverine. Why was it so hard to put that fear aside? Put it aside and love this man. She scrunched her lips in regret.

They lay that way for awhile as the candles burned lower and cast longer shadows on the pictures adorning the walls. Time was inconsequential. Only the warmth of his body, the strength of his arms and the tenderness of his breath consoled her.

Then she felt the familiar stirrings of his maleness. Julia-Rae reached behind her and caressed his thigh. He throbbed in return.

"Make love to me again," she begged. "Oh I will, I don't want this night to end." "Neither do I." she replied.

Roy reached over and pulled another plastic package from the drawer. "Give me a moment, to clean up first, I'll be right back." Roy kissed her on the cheek and walked out.

Roy strode out, his delicious rear was the last Julia-Rae saw as he disappeared from the room. She reached over to get a sip from the wine glass she had left behind. The top drawer still lay open and there glinting in the candlelight lay, half exposed a book. Not just any book, she knew, but what looked like a romance. It was hard to mistake the couple clutching at each other on the cover and the look of love in their eyes. She hadn't seen many, or read any, since her grandma had read them to her.

"Odd thing for a man to possess."

No sign of Roy yet. Like in a dream she reached for the book and pulled it free from its slumber. Colorado Weekend. Her curiosity aroused Julia-Rae opened the book and saw the handwritten inscription written in delicate handwriting inside. It looked so much like another woman's handwriting.

"To Ray, Thanks for all of those hot passionate nights spent in enjoyment of you, this book and the nights to come. Love Angie."

The date scrawled in the same slow soft style was only five days ago.

The book fell from her bloodless hands at the same time Roy strode back into the room clutching the packet in his hand.

The words had already etched a permanent brand in her heart. He had lied, he had been with another, only a few days ago and quite intimately at that.

Roy stared at the book falling to the floor, "What are you doing going through my stuff?"

"What the hell is this Roy?"

Roy stopped in midstride the foil packet fell from his fingers. The rage brewing on her face wasn't lost on the candles glow. "It's nothing, it's just a book."

He couldn't explain the reason for the book. It would mean exposing Mrs. Leighton and eventually Carrie and Sean. Reality, his past reality, slammed at Roy with the suddenness of a brick wall meeting a speeding locomotive.

"From a lover damn it. You told me you hadn't anyone in your life for quite awhile. I guess five days means awhile to you then, doesn't it Roy." Julia-Rae wanted to rip that book from all shred of existence, from your memories. Why couldn't she just go on with life and love him? Her teeth groaned from grinding together under the anger that threatened to spill over. She wanted to rifle that hideous book at him. As if that would somehow erase it from reality. A new, harsher reality that had just crept in the open door like a summer thunderstorm sweeps the still prairies before it. The hard familiar walls of rage were in place. Yet for once in her life Julia-Rae stopped herself from wanting to scream and tear him apart. She picked up the book and dropped it into the drawer like a disease.

“It’s not what it seems.”

“Oh, it isn’t, then tell me Roy what those words written by another woman’s hand means, seems pretty explicit to me.”

He stood there speechless, looking like he was struggling to say what was on his mind, but finally, couldn’t. “I can’t explain right now, you have no right to snoop through my stuff.”

Yes, she knew she had broken some scared code by snooping through his stuff.

“Snoop? You left the damn drawer open. Roy I need an explanation here.” Please, dear God let there be some reason, some valid reason for this book. She fought to quell the tide of seething anger. Every heartbeat sent stabbing little daggers to her heart. Ripping at it with their jagged dull blades, mangling all within, leaving no prisoners. Leaving Julia-Rae with no energy to tear at him. She just wanted to get out, get out and get away from this man that she had fallen in love with.

"I-I can't tell you Julia-Rae. You better get out now." He couldn't tell her about Angie, Carrie and Sean. The air of the bedroom swirled around him and through him like he was a straw scarecrow stuck into the cold earth of the prairie. He continued standing there as Julia-Rae hurriedly dressed. Tension, cold and solid, sealed his lips. Her face told him all as she stormed by. Tears streamed down her face. Please don't say anything, he thought and she didn't have to; the look on her face spoke more then the contents of the holy bible. Betrayal and slime. Blunt and to the point, seared into his vision.

Why even angry did she look so beautiful? The slam of the front door let him know she was gone. Roy stood there, head bowed, as the reverberation of the door echoed in the background. Roy sank into the confines of his bed. He could smell the cloying scent of Julia-Rae's perfume.

Orchids, white empty orchids. Everything in his life had just come to a grinding halt. Roy pulled the romance book from the drawer and stared at the cover. The teeth of that tiger he'd been riding all of these years glinted back at him, as its jaws closed around him. The jaws of what he'd been doing to Julia-Rae and the razor-sharpness of the past tore at Roy. Roy closed his eyes sobbing and let merciful sleep wash over him.

Tears streamed down Julia-Rae's face as she rode the elevator back down to her car. She didn't even think she picked up her panties or bra. Bastard, let him keep those as a memento. That's about all he's every going to get from me now. I can't believe I could be so stupid. A glance in the reflection of the elevators metal walls told her hair was disheveled and her makeup was running down her cheeks. She wasn't even certain if she had her dress on properly. It all didn't matter, none of that mattered, what counted was her heart. This was how her relationship to her last boyfriend Mark had ended. They had been school sweethearts, for the last five years, they had become very close and over the years he had grown to become her best friend. Mark had proposed to her and everything. But there was one thing he hadn't shared with her. An affair he was having with a girl named Samantha. Julia-Rae came over to Mark's one day to surprise him for his birthday by getting dressed up in something very sexy and waiting for him on his bed. It was while she was rummaging around for candles that she found the notes Samantha had left him. Notes extolling his male virtues, ones Julia-Rae was quite familiar with. What had really hurt was when she confronted him and he denied nothing. The idea of living with someone who could screw around on her was not Julia-Rae's idea of a partner in life. The heart ached then and old scars tore open again leaving ugly jagged wounds. She cried all the way home to her small one-bedroom condo.

There were messages on her answering machine, probably his, she couldn't bare to hear his voice right now.

It had been five long years since that day, it would be probably longer before she got involved again especially after what happened with Tim. Were all men bastards?

Damn, why didn't she just stick to business, at least it was safe there, at least one could put their heart into it and not get it spit back at you skewered on a dagger still beating cut into a million little pieces. Julia-Rae hugged the three foot high teddy bear that her parents had given her when she was born. It was the last thing her mom had bought for her before going into the hospital to have her. It was all she had for a memory.

"Oh Freddie, just hold me and never let me go, promise." Julia-Rae cried herself to sleep on her old friend. How many nights as a child did she cry herself to sleep in the same manner, wishing she had a mom to call her own?

Roy sat in silence the next morning. The vast emptiness of the condo was unending. A huge naked void and he was there floating in the center. He had tried calling Antonio but had got no response. He wanted Antonio to stop what he was about to do. He knew Antonio would be making moves already this morning. He didn't waste much in the way of time, the man had the ruthlessness of hundreds of years of Mafioso blood running through him. He would be pulling out all stops.

Roy sat staring at the flickering of the gas fireplace. Scents of orchids hung in the air, cloying bitter reminders. The two of them kissing, her wineglass still sat on the mantel. Lipstick adorned the edge. Her lipstick from her lips, the same lips he had kissed and wanted to be kissing again.

He sighed. Her smile, her eyes full of passion and live for him. One moment she had been there and the next she was gone.

Roy knew he had to stop what Antonio was doing. He couldn't go on with this and hurt her more than he already had. He knew how Antonio would take this; as a stab in the back. Over a woman of all things, he was prepared to turn his back on his friend. Roy shook his head. What was so special about her?

Her eyes, her smile, the craziness she possessed inside, so much like his. Roy stared into the flames, maybe Mrs. Leighton was right. For the first time in the last eight years he was falling in love. Falling in love with the woman that he was supposed to be befriending in order to take over her company. Damn. This wasn't part of the plot.

Roy stared at the cover of the romance novel Mrs. Leighton had scrawled in. He had a few of them, over the years she had made notes in several of the novels he had read her. It had never dawned on him that someone would ever read them and get the wrong impression. A small smile light his face, she was one crazy old lady, so much like Helen

Lavoie at the nursing home. So much like Carrie had been also. So much like Julia-Rae is. Or was. Well he had lost her, there was only one thing left to do. He picked up the phone.

Chapter Eleven

Julia-Rae knew something was wrong when she had to unlock the door to her office when she got in. There were two notes pinned to the door, along with a huge basket of roses, no doubt from that wretched excuse for a man, Roy. The events of last night had left her feeling like a bridge a day after the deluge had gone by. A channel drained of water; stone washed away. What else could go wrong she didn't know, but dealing with a sob letter from him would probably the least of her worries she was certain.

The letter was from Roy and it wasn't a sob I'll do anything please forgive me letter like she had thought. It simply said, "If you want an answer to the writing on the book buzz #B12 8319-103st at 8:00 tonight. Don't worry, I won't be there, there's someone you have to meet." He obviously had something up his sleeve. Julia-Rae played with the card for a second and then slid it into her purse. Normally she wouldn't have bothered to waste the time of the day on the guy. Yet something puzzled her and at the same time intrigued her.

>I'll think about it.< She texted him and shut her phone off. Julia-Rae knew she had far larger worries at the moment.

She opened the other letter, it wasn't what she suspected. A resignation letter from Cindy. She had quit. She had an offer from another magazine, they were offering her double her salary and benefits. Effective immediately. She had made arrangements to have a temp come in this afternoon to help out. The word sorry appeared no less then five times. Julia-Rae understood, she'd have done the same if it wasn't her company. Damn. The phones were ringing fast and furious up front, Julia-Rae let the automatic answering machine take them. She hadn't the heart or stomach to deal with anymore at the moment. She sank back into her chair, the full effects of the letter hitting home. "Damn, double damn." She read Cindy's letter again. Catatonia reigned supreme.

Julia-Rae jumped at a loud knock on her door.

"Ms. McNaughton?" Spoke the cool confident voice of Antonio Rufuko. "I made an appointment to see you this morning, but it appears your secretary isn't available to let me in, so I let myself in."

They were probably the ones who had bought her out, she thought. Julia-Rae hadn't checked the appointment sheet to verify if he was supposed to be here or not. It really didn't matter. She noticed he didn't extend his hand in greeting this time. Shaking the hand of a snake wasn't something she'd do willingly anyway. "How can I help you, Mr. Rufuko?"

"I have brought a new proposal to you, one I'm sure you'll find a little more to your liking."

He withdrew a sheaf of papers slowly, like a gunslinger unholstering his gun, she thought. Heat hit her cheeks as he laid the papers on her desk.

"I realize you'll want time to review them with your lawyer before signing. However, would you like me to go over the new terms with you?"

"Terms? Not another word out of those greasy, snake lips of yours. Mr. Rufuko drop those papers and the only thing that would give me any pleasure right now other then holding a gun in my hands and thank God for you I'm not PMSing, is the back of your head exiting my office."

"Well if I can help in. . ."

She had it, how she held her temper this long Julia-Rae didn't know. "Get the hell out of my office!"

A slight smile lit his usually sterile face as he slowly turned to leave. "I'll be expecting your call then?"

“Expect this!” Julia-Rae grabbed a box of paperclips and flung them at the door as he hurriedly closed it behind him.

An explosion of glittering silver clips littered the air before splattering across the carpet.

“Damn.” She screamed. Julia-Rae stood there for long moments clenching her teeth together. Damn cool son-of-a-bitch he was. The phones up front kept ringing incessantly. Julia-Rae plopped back into her chair. She wanted to put her hands over her face and cry. “Damn, I’ve no time for self-pity. The temp should be here soon.” She grabbed a blank paper and began to think of what she’d need to tell the girl. Basically everything. Julia-Rae grabbed the flowers, pitched them into the trash. She picked up the papers Antonio left behind. The numbers scrawled on them caught her eye. She stopped for a moment and glanced at the details. Reasonable wasn’t the word, this new offer was more than double the previous one.

What I'd give to have that bastard's two-timing body next to mine right about now, holding me, She thought. Why did I have to snoop in his stuff? Better now than later. Angie, that woman's name burned into her memory. I'll scratch her bloody eyes out if I ever met her. On the other hand maybe she did me a massive favor.

Still Roy's experience in this type of matter would be indispensable right now. No, this was her battle, hers to go alone. First she had to find out about this Stanza group and if they had indeed hired Cindy away from her. Somehow she sensed what the answer would be.

There was a light knock on her office door. "Ms. McNaughton, I'm Trish from the office temp services. Cindy called us to come in this morning and help you out. Oh, I see you've had a paperclip incident."

"Could say that. Good, I'll show you what you'll need to do to get started. You've got great timing."

After that she'd phone her dad and see if he could meet her for lunch on the weekend. She reached in her pocket for a Kleenex and pulled out the card instead. Julia-Rae stared at the card for a long moment wanting to crumple it up and toss it into the trash, like him. What in the world was he up to? Ordinarily she couldn't be bothered to give the time of day to him or any man. But he was no ordinary man. There was so much of her soul tied in with his. Maybe that was one of the problems she spent so much time working she never had taken the time to sit down and enjoy life and the pleasures of a man in her life. Or was it simply that she was too scared to get hurt, like her dad had been?

The pain of last night needled at her with wicked, ragged dirty edges like cut glass. Too late, she already been hurt and she knew the pain had only begun to sink in. Julia-Rae thrust the card back in her pocket, she had lots to do here before leaving tonight. It was far safer to bury herself in her work.

“Come on in dearie, you must be Julia-Rae.”

The elderly lady’s voice on the intercom startled Julia-Rae. What she was expecting coming here she didn’t know. But that voice, in archaic English accents so much like her grandmas, somehow wasn’t it. The apartment building was one of the older buildings in the Whyte Avenue of south Edmonton. The area had in recent history given its shoddy old rundown image away to revamped condos, yuppie homes and the nearby university crowd, with its attached eclectic young folk. The refurbished old four storey apartment complex had probably started life out as someone’s mansion many years ago. Julia-Rae entered and walked up the creaking oak stairs. An ornate elevator, complete with brass bars and fifties tastes sat off to one side. Julia-Rae wanted to use the solid wooden stairs, they held so much wealth and class that one couldn’t help but feel privileged to be walking up the steps. She stopped before the door of B12. Beautiful rug lined the hall with its red Winchester designs, solidly English in character. A picture of flowers hung in the hallway and well cared for rubber plants set in wicker pots on each side of the door. A building with character and charm. She only hoped whoever was inside was the same.

Julia-Rae hesitated, before knocking, wondering if turning around and leaving wasn't perhaps the wiser thing to do.

"Do come on in, Dearie, the doors open."

Cautiously Julia-Rae entered. The only other person that had ever called her dearie had been her grandma. The apartment wasn't overly large, but it was well done in antique furnishings. This person was or had been well to do. Numerous china figurines lined the walls and in the china cabinets.

"They're in need of a good cleaning I realize, but do come in, Roy has told me much about you."

Julia-Rae closed the door, wondering how she could have known what she was thinking. She turned and finally spotted the elderly looking lady sitting by a window in a rocking chair. The frail looking lady, while looking distinguished, had the look of someone who had lived their life and was now waiting to expire.

"Sit here beside me dear, heavens knows I don't bite, hell even my false teeth have fallen out," she smirked.

Julia-Rae smiled and sat in the padded chair beside the old lady. On the coffee table before them sat an elegant sterling silver platter, two silver spoons, a delicate china teapot, with many cracks running splintered through it and butter cookies sat piled in precise order on the platter. Two teacups completed the setting. The annoyingly small kind, Julia-Rae hated as a child that her grandma had always used. The ones that could only fit two fingers and one had to sip very patiently. Something she was always short of when she was young. The smell of strong English tea wafted into the air. “Hi, I’m Angie Leighton.”

“Julia-Rae McNaughton.” Angie? It was the same name as on the book. Could it be?

“My goodness I’d recognize you anywhere. Why that hair is indeed as Roy said, kissed by the hand of St. Elmos fire. Are the curls natural?”

“Unfortunately, yes. I always wanted straight hair, preferably brunette.” The padded arms of the old chair were very comforting. The lady and the apartment reminded her so much of her grandma. “The tea smells wonderful, Mrs. Leighton.”

“Well, it isn’t meant for smelling, this is a drinking tea, not a sniffing one. Go ahead and pour yourself a cup.”

Julia-Rae giggled; it was becoming evident the old girl had quite the sense of humor. “Would you like one also?”

"Yes, just half though, no sugar, I've had a couple today and its sent the old heart a ticking."

"Oh, do you have heart troubles?"

"Dearie, can I call you JR?"

"Yes," my grandma did. She wanted to add but didn't.

"At my age I've more plastic parts put into me then real ones. Every time someone turns on one of those microwaves my left leg goes limp."

Julia-Rae giggled again, beginning to finally relax.

"And besides I haven't got my husband around anymore to waste a pounding heart on."

"Oh, Mrs. Leighton, you're incorrigible. Any children?" She wanted to add what have you to do with scum bucket Roy. But thought the old gal would get to it eventually. Anyways she was enjoying her company.

"A son who lives out East someplace, who I last saw ten years ago or so."

"Does he call?"

"Call? Heartless bugger, if Canada Post had to depend on him for

a living they'd be under years ago. No, he hasn't wrote or called since I can remember when. I also had a daughter."

"Had, she also doesn't write?"

"No, where she is she can't write." She pointed to the heavens with a shaky finger.

"Oh I'm so sorry. Now let me hear a little about you and your relation to Roy."

"My father is Bill McNaughton, the accounting firm. My mom died at birth."

"Heaven, God rest her soul."

Those words were like honey in cough syrup. Very comforting. "You know that's a phrase my very English granny used all the time.

She raised me as a child."

“Your father?”

“Well, when he was home he spent a lot of time with me, but he buried himself in his work. Never remarried or hardly dated.”

“Good looker.”

“Very handsome man.”

“Ah, what a waste. My husband passed away twelve years ago and if I could find anyone interested in this carcass of bones and plastic joints, I’d a scooped them up and found out just what kind of speed silicone takes and how long before it wore out. Life’s too damn short you know.”

“Mrs. Leighton?” Did she just hear that, from the old girl’s lips?

“So, tell me, did you really smack Roy on the butt on your first date.”

“What first date?” For a second the internal firebomb went off.

“Hah, its okay I was just kidding, hah, Roy was right you do have the fire to match your hair. A woman with passion. I like that. Had a bit of that myself when I was younger.”

“Say, how do you know Roy anyway?”

“Oh… ah, let’s just say he’s an old friend of the family. I’ve known him since he was knee high to a grasshopper. A good man, strong,

passionate, just like the kind you read in the books.”

“What books?”

“Those romance ones, like the kind I gave him that you stumbled into at his place. I’m sorry if I got him into trouble.”

“It’s okay really.”

“Can you humor this old gal and before you go read me a chapter? I can’t see the print anymore, at least not without glasses so thick I’d either get whiplash wearing them or fall over and break my neck.”

"Sure, I'd love to." This was all too weird. This was what Roy was hiding? That he goes to an old lady's house and reads romance books to her? Why couldn't he have told her that last night? Somehow her intuition told her there was more here than that. It didn't ring with total truth.

Julia-Rae read the next chapter to Angie. She set the book down. The hero and heroine were falling wildly in love with each other. Was that how she was feeling about this man? All of those crazy torturous things from the heart. The answer thudded in back of her throat. Julia-Rae closed the book. "I've got to go now." She rose to leave. "Thanks for the tea, I had a wonderful time."

"Thanks for the company, come again, I can see why Ray … er Roy likes you. I'd like to spend more time together if you're interested and I'm always welcome to have someone read to me."

"Anytime I've really enjoyed myself. Here let me put away the tea for you."

"It's okay, really you don't."

"Never mind, you brought out the tea, the least I can do is put it away."

Julia-Rae picked up the tea set and walked into the kitchen. On her way back to the living room she saw a framed picture of a younger looking Roy, a gorgeous blonde lady and a toddler.

"Mrs. Leighton, that picture of Roy, is that also your daughter?" She asked returning to the living room.

"Ah… ah yes and the boy is… er her son." She said caught off guard.

"Son? You never mentioned a grandson."

"Well, you never asked." Mrs. Leighton's voice rose, sounding perturbed. "Look I'm feeling pretty tired, I really need to lay down and rest."

It was obvious to Julia-Rae that Mrs. Leighton was suddenly playing avoidance. "Well, maybe we'll talk more on my next visit."

“Right-o dearie, now run along.” She yawned, in what looked to Julia-Rae as a very fake attempt.

As Julia-Rae walked out she knew something here just wasn’t right. Perhaps it was the way Roy was looking at the lady in the picture. Why was that picture in the kitchen, it looked so out of place there. It belonged on the living room mantel. But there was more to this story, of that she was certain. But for the moment she had far bigger worries and it had been one helluva day. Time for a relaxing bubble bath and some quiet music, probably Mozart, before meeting her dad tomorrow.

It was lunch at the Paridisio Café, except being the weekend there were no business suits dining around them. The café managed to usually attract the weekday business crowd. There were only a few other couples around at the moment, all dressed in more casual wear. Julia-Rae was actually glad it was quieter it gave her more freedom to chat.

"So I went to this little old ladies apartment yesterday dad. I thought she was a secret lover of Roy's and she turned out to be nearly eighty years old. God, do I ever feel foolish."

"Old lady? Have you talked to Roy yet?"

"No I haven't."

"That's good. Would this old lady happen to be Mrs. Angie Leighton?"

Julia-Rae knew her mouth had hit the table and would probably have been rolling around on the floor gathering discarded breadcrumbs if she hadn't slapped a hand over her mouth. "Ah, how could you possibly have known?"

"Well since we chatted last I did a little digging. The name Stanza group rang a bit of a bell with me. I used to have as one of my accounts Bill Sutfield who was in those days running a fledgling magazine and newspaper business. He had two sons, Jeremiah and Ray. When he passed away his sons took over the company. They allowed themselves to merge with a group of investors and the new company, which

I found out just the other day, was the Stanza group of magazines. Jeremiah sold the majority of his shares and moved on. Ray is still president but in absence. The boys I never dealt with much, although I heard Ray was a little more aggressive of the two and had better business sense then Jeremiah." He stopped to sip some sparkling water.

"President in absence, what do mean? Has he disappeared or something?"

"Well kind of, most of this story had been kept hush hush. Old man Bill had quite a bit of pull with certain fellas."

"Pull? What would he need to have pull on?"

"Well Bill also had a very reputable background and close contacts with major religious types in town. Jeremiah moved to Winnipeg and Ray married Carrie Leighton. As far as I know they had a son."

"Oh my God, Mrs. Leighton's daughter. But Carrie's dead, Angie told me herself."

“Yes, she is, Ray as quite a heavy drinker, this part I just found out about just recently. Ray apparently drove home drunk one night and got in a car accident. Carrie died before he got out of the hospital.”

“And let me guess if this was made public knowledge old man Bill’s reputation would have gone down the tubes.”

“Big time, he had aspirations of running for mayor of this town at one time.”

“His son?”

“Ray? He survived but I don’t know what happened to him.”

“No, Ray’s son.”

“I’ve a car, as soon as we’re done lunch instead of explaining I’ll show you his son.”

Julia-Rae sat in silence the rest of lunch; she knew better then try to pry something out of her dad once he had his mind set on not talking any further. Could this all be true? As they drove over to another part of south Edmonton it hit

Julia-Rae, hadn't she heard Mrs. Leighton accidentally say Ray instead of Roy. Could this Roy, or Ray be the same man? Roy never touched a drop of booze in the whole time they were together. Was that the reason?

They pulled up to the Mt. Pleasant Nursing Home. Julia-Rae walked with a slow steady stiffness. Her body was slowly becoming a cold, emotionless shell. Too much was happening, too fast.

"Let me guess, we've really come to see old man Sutfield."

"No my dear, I wish this was as easy as that. The old man died of a massive heart attack about nine years ago. I figured this you'd want to see for yourself. They normally wouldn't let us waltz in here, but the Good Samaritan Nursing Home Society is also one of my accounts so I can ask for a few favors."

As they walked down the sterile corridors Julia-Rae watched the blank, aged faces that stared from the frail bodies sitting in the chairs lining the halls. Would that be her someday? Just souls trapped in shells, unwilling to let go. About as unwilling as she was to let go of the idea that Roy Sutter and Ray Sutfield were one and the same. And if they were what did that mean to her? How could she have fallen in love for the same man trying to buy out her company; unless-

She swallowed hard. Had this all been a ploy, had she been duped? And if she had, why did Roy let her come to see Mrs. Leighton. Did he care enough for her that he was willing to show her the truth about his past and risk losing her forever? They exited the back of the building and entered the gardens. She walked in silence beside her dad, wanting more then anything to just bolt and run to the safety of her condo.

Just ahead of them were two people, one was in a wheelchair and the other appeared to be an elderly blonde with a wavy hairdo probably hair sprayed galore like a lot of the older women did. She was dressed in the brightest yellow dress she had seen in a long time. The lady leaned back and laughed a full, rich laugh. She didn't have to talk to this person to know she was beyond a doubt the most alive person in this place. She was probably more alive then the staff.

It was when they got within a few feet that Julia-Rae finally noticed the person sitting in the wheelchair. It was a young boy, probably ten or so. One side of his face hung limply, it was very apparent that he was disabled and unable to walk. The loose curls of blonde hair grabbed her attention. Any doubts were immediately erased. His young features bore an uncanny resemblance to Roy.

"Is that from the accident?" "Yes," her dad soberly replied.

"Hi," said the elderly lady with a sparkle to her voice that belayed years from her, "you must be Mr. McNaughton and this?" She extended her hand.

"This is Julia-Rae, my daughter."

They shook hands. "I'm Helen Lavoie and this is Sean Sutfield." Helen pointed to the boy who perked up at his name.

"H-hi, did you bring my daddy?" A smile spread across his face and eagerness lit his eyes. Julia-Rae recognized the smile in his eyes, she had seen it many times before on Roy's face. The lad obviously loved his father very much.

Julia-Rae squatted before the lad. "No, I'm afraid he's not here with us. But I'm here, does your daddy come visit you often?"

"Yes," Helen answered. "Usually once a week when he's not out on a business trip somewhere."

"Oh, your hair, its on fire!" Sean squealed.

"No it's not on fire, it's colored that way naturally." The humor was unmistakable, he was Roy's son.

What pain had this man endured in the last few years? Yet he still came and visited his son. It was obvious that he loved him deeply. Julia-Rae allowed her dad to put his arm around her as they walked back to the car.

"Oh dad, what have I got myself involved with?"

"I don't know my dear, but I do know this, as soon as I found out

I thought you needed to know before it got too late."

"Thanks dad, I love you very much, but it's already too late. I've fallen very much in love with this man." The same man that was driving her crazy was also part of trying to buy her out. Tears splattered the sidewalk as they walked. Her dad said not another word as he held her against him as they walked.

As they drove back to her place Julia-Rae sat staring at the papers Antonio gave her yesterday. The spot where her name resided stared blankly back.

"Damn him."

There was only one way to know if he truly loved her or this was all a magnificent plot to get everything away from her.

Her hands shook as she reached for the pen in her pocket. Tears fell onto the document. “Take me to Roy’s condo dad.”

“Why? Don’t tell me you’re willing to risk everything for what?

For this man who’s a drunk, whose actions lead to the death of his wife and crippling of their son.”

“Dad I can’t explain it, you don’t feel what I feel in his arms or the look in his eyes. Besides I’ve seen what he’s done since then and you yourself said to go for it, let someone into my life.”

Silence pervaded the air between them. Julia-Rae knew those words had struck at her dad as hard as a slap across the face. “Look dad, I’m sorry. I need to do what I feel I must. If that means taking a huge risk, then I will.”

“Apology accepted, I guess just know this my dear. No matter what happens in life you’ll always be my little girl and I’ll always love you.”

“Thanks dad, you’ve raised me to grow up strong and independent, sometimes that’s interfered with allowing someone into my life, I know that. But you’ve also shown me that no matter what in life I did, you’d always be there for me.”

“Yah like the time you dug up all the flowers in our backyard and planted them upside down wanting to see if they’d grow to China.”

“And you watered those things for a week before you showed me, they were dead.”

They both laughed.

“Yes, my dear do what you feel you must, I’ll be here.” “Thanks Dad.”

Chapter Twelve

"Here." Julia-Rae handed the documents to Roy two days later. It had taken a courier to get to him and set up this appointment. He stood just inside the door to his condo looking disheveled and more. His eyes bore a cold, withdrawn look. He'd not shaved in a couple of day and looked like he'd been drinking, but his breath held no sour alcohol induced fumes.

"What are these?"

"Don't look so surprised, Mr. Ray Sutfield. These are the papers that snake-skinned lawyer of yours Mr. Rofuko asked me to sign. You want my company, you've got it, enjoy." The fire in her voice left an acrid taste in her mouth. Please dear god, she thought, tell me that he really wants me and not my company. Even standing there with sorrow written all over a face she was so used to seeing full of life and not drained, so empty. Yet, even depleted he still looked handsome in whiskers; a hint of his cologne hung about him. "Oh, I guess you figured it out."

"Yah, I figured out that you're nothing more than a sophisticated con artist. And to think I had some strong feelings for you."

"I don't know what to say, I never really wanted to hurt you."

"Hurt me? You've hurt me more than anyone has ever hurt me before. Goodbye Ray Sutfield."

Julia-Rae turned and very slowly walked down the corridor, each echoing step drumming the memory of the man she had begun to fall in love away from the hurtful corridors of her soul. Praying he'd say or do something, call out to her and want to be with her. Hold her and say he cared for her.

Only the echoes and the silence broke the sanctity of the hallway as Julia-Rae entered the elevator and turned around. The last thing she saw as the doors closed, was Ray standing papers in hand hanging limply by his side. The thud of the elevator's doors reverberated in her heart. As a wave of anguish sent a flood of tears earthward, Julia-Rae understood why her dad had never got involved with anyone after her mother died. She understood only too well.

Roy walked into the boardroom. There were twelve others sitting around the large desk. All were men he knew for many years all were men who admired and respected Roy as a leader. He was late. Roy had a hard time getting ready for this meeting. Antonio rose and shook his hand, "good to see you, Roy."

"Same Antonio, it's been too long awhile." He hadn't told Antonio, or anyone here about the papers Julia-Rae gave him two days ago. Roy placed his briefcase on the desk.

"You don't look too well, my friend."

Roy just smiled limply at Antonio. The others, all dressed in suits, sat chatting with one another. He had a moment. “No, I didn’t

Antonio. I need to talk to you privately before we begin.” The two excused themselves and stepped into the hallway.

“What’s up?”

“Before we start, I need to know what the intent of this company would be to Ms. McNaughton and her company if we were to get her consent in securing this deal.”

“Someone we trust would be placed in a position of authority to oversee all aspects of the company and eventually we’d phase her out or absorb the whole magazine into our line.”

The image of a bird, wings clipped, hopelessly flapping around, trying to fly and unable, shocked Ray. That was to be the fate of Julia-Rae. She wouldn’t accept it, she’d die if she was caged up. Ray shook his head, “I see.”

Antonio looked straight at Ray. Straight into his eyes and into the face of a long-time friend, a man he trusted and respected, “You have the papers signed don’t you?”

Ray sighed, “Yes I do, and now I know what must be done.”

“Good, lets go back in and get this meeting started.”

Roy strode to the head of the desk. “Gentlemen, I call this meeting to order.”

Antonio read off the minutes of the last meeting. The proposed financial projections for the next quarter (and they looked pretty dismal). Then he turned to Ray.

“However, gentlemen, I believe Ray has something we wants to add to this meeting.”

“As a matter of fact, I do. Gentlemen I have enjoyed the time here as president and believe I’ve made a great deal of progress and profit for Stanza Enterprises, but I do believe its time someone else runs this ship. Someone with more hands-on business knowledge and someone willing to put

100% effort into the leadership helm of Stanza. I have elected to resign and wish to nominate Antonio Rofuko as the new acting president." Ray opened up his briefcase and pulled the letter he typed up last night from under the documents Julia-Rae had signed.

Antonio peered into the case and saw her handwritten autograph scrawled on the papers. He looked at Ray and leaned over, "I hope she's worth it Ray."

"I know she's worth it Antonio." Ray pulled the resignation paper from his briefcase and put in on the table.

"Gentlemen, its time someone is here that will run the company all of the time. I trust that you'll look after the terms of my severance as quickly as possible. Thank you." Ray handed the documents to Antonio, shook his hand and walked out.

The sound of twelve jaws hitting the oak table sent a resounding thud that echoed through the corridors for the rest of the day. "When you make a decision to do something, just go ahead and do it immediately. Before someone tries to talk you out of it. Hit them hard and fast." Words his dad had left him. Now he just had to find the courage to talk to Julia-Rae. There was a voice mail message on his car phone when he got back to meet Mrs. Leighton.

Julia-Rae sat quietly in the living room of Mrs. Leighton's apartment. She stared at the handwritten note she had received from the older lady. The note said to meet her here at 3:00 for tea. Julia-Rae waited patiently. The old gal had left another note saying she was out to pickup some sugar and she'd be right back, a neighbor had let her in. How the old gal got around Julia-Rae wasn't quite sure but apparently, she still did.

The picture of Roy, Carrie and Sean sat on the mantel in the living room. Tears welled up, she had really fallen for this guy, would have probably even become his wife if he would have asked. All gone now.

A click at the door, Julia-Rae turned and went to open it expecting to find a tired and thankful Mrs. Leighton and nearly fell into the arms of the man in the picture.

"Julia-Rae? What are you doing here?"

"I might ask you the same question, buster." Her cheeks flushed, she had nearly forgotten how handsome he was and how she wanted to jump into those arms.

"I'm sorry, I didn't know you'd be here."

His cologne, his nearness and that virile male electricity reached out, pulling at her. Why was he so impossible to resist?

"I'll leave and come back later if you're visiting." Yet Roy stood there, immobile. His feet were begging him to run, to flee before it got ugly. His heart hammered him to the spot. The sunlight peering through the windows highlighted her red hair. The anger that flashed continuously in those brown eyes, lit afire by the red tresses of curled hair. Such passion, such zest and life.

"Ah, no stay." She backed up a couple of steps. "Besides, Mrs. Leighton isn't here. I thought you were her."

Roy walked in slowly, like Indiana Jones entering the Temple of Doom. His face bore a rigid, be prepared for anything look that his dad often had going into meetings. "If I'm going to be yelled at again, I'll not stand here and put up with it. By the way where is Angie, I've haven't seen her leave this place in many years, although I'm sure she must."

"She left a message for me to meet her here at 3:00 and when I got here there's another note saying she's stepped out for a few minutes to grab some sugar."

"Funny I got the same letter to meet her here for coffee."

"Obviously the old gal staged this whole thing. If what you're telling me is the truth and there isn't much I'd believe coming from those lips."

Roy's face bore a cold distant look. "Before you say anything I do want to say that you don't have to worry about

Stanza taking over, I've resigned and torn up the documents you gave me."

"You did what?" She was dumbfounded. "But why, you had everything you wanted."

"Yeah, I had everything I realized everything except for the one thing I really wanted."

"And what was that?" Her heart thudded to a stop. "Now if this is a pity party you can take it and stick it where the midnight sun never sets."

Roy's face sagged. He thought about the events of the last few days. "No, it's not like that. I realized last night that all of those insane, passionate quirks that are Julia-Rae McNaughton are all values that I admire and cherish. I mean it dawned on me by the company I keep. Mrs. Leighton and Helen, both crazy women that still have that spark of life and zaniness about them. I often said to Helen, if she was forty years younger, I'd jump at the chance to date her and probably marry her. Well, the realization hit me that the younger version of that lady is standing right here in this room. I admit what I did was wrong, terribly wrong. I know your opinion of me is extremely low."

"Low, you probably have to look up to see cockroaches crawling by on the sidewalk."

"The truth is," Roy swallowed hard, if he really wanted this woman now was the time to put all the cards on the table, game time was over. "I did originally approach you with the intent to seduce you hopefully sidetracking you into taking over your business."

Both stared.

"What I didn't expect to do," he swallowed, the words sticking to his throat like molasses, "was to be attracted to you and. . ." he hesitated. Roy stared into the ceiling seeking to speak the words he needed. Struggling not to tear at the thought of a lifetime spent without her. "The truth is I didn't expect to fall in love with you," he sighed. "So I've quit as president, the company is going to buy out my shares and I'm going to disappear for awhile. I need to think about things, about myself. One thing you did for me was make me realize I've got feelings and some pretty deep ones around my past and around you."

"Feelings about Carrie's death? And the crippling of Sean."

"You know about that?" Roy took a step back. His whole world had suddenly stopped while the rest of the world kept right on spinning.

"Yes, my dad is Dennis McNaughton of McNaughton Accountants. Your dad Bill Sutfield was one of his customers. He did some digging and found out about your name change and the story behind why it happened. I know about Carrie, the alcohol and what happened that night. I also went to visit Sean at the nursing home. That's why you changed your name isn't it, Ray Sutfield?"

"Yes, I couldn't let anyone find out I had tarnished the company name and my dad's name because of what I had done. I had disgraced myself. I made a vow to myself to never touch another drop of alcohol after that. But I couldn't bring back Carrie or reverse what happened to Sean."

"So you've been basically hiding out all this time. Packing a whole load of baggage."

"In some respect I guess yes. I still managed the Stanza group of companies, actually the merge happened about the same time as my accident and things worked out quite well. No one questioned an absentee president. Especially when Antonio manages it so well when I'm not there." Roy turned slightly, trying to fight off the tear that struggled to break free. "You know every time I go to see him it tears open my heart, even after all of these years."

"Yes, I thought about that and the pain that it must bring is tremendous. But you know what I admire after I met Sean, was that you still go to see him nearly every week. Most men that didn't care would have locked him away and not bothered to show up." "He's still my son." Roy blurted.

Julia-Rae saw the brief spark of fury under those dark and mysterious eyes. Was that what he saw every time she got upset? “Visiting Sean made me realize that under that hard exterior beats the heart of a passionate and caring man. A man that has also come to mean more to me then I even realized. Trust right now is a big issue for me, especially after I found out about what you did and what you were trying to do. Yet, my dad made me realize that I’ve shoved everyone away from me and kept people away trying to not get hurt like he was after my mom died. I became too much like him and that hurt too. That’s something you made you realize and the fact that I’m scared, deathly scared of letting a man into my life.”

“After the accident I locked up most of my feelings, I didn’t want anyone to get close to me again. I never thought I’d run into someone as crazy and spontaneous, so much like me, again. I never expected this to happen, this was supposed to be just a business move. Only after I stared at those papers you handed me did I realize that I got what I wanted. Everything except for the one thing that I really wanted, after I ripped up the papers it dawned on me that the only thing I wanted was you. The only thing I couldn't have, whether I go through with the deal or not, was you. Antonio was right, he saw that I was attracted to you."

"What, after all you've done. After all of the stress, anger and hurt you've caused me. Me with this wild headstrong temper."

"That you use to keep people away. At least I'll admit to my demons and live with the consequences of my actions. You. . . you just run and hide. Afraid to. . ."

Truth's fire licked at her as Julia-Rae tore from his grip and spun away. "Go to hell and get out of my life. You've done nothing but destroy it." She gulped twice like a guppy out of water, unable for once in her life to find any further words to fire back at him. She stormed into the bathroom to grab some tissue as tears streamed down her face. He'd torn past all of those barriers she had erected to keep her safe in her life and thrown her naked on the beach of her life and was still hurting her. No one had ever done that before and the worst part was that he was right, damn it. He had cut straight to the bone and somewhere in her heart little splinters began to tear away with unbelievable agony. Truth was, as hard as it took to admit, as she stared into the pitiful face looking back at her in the bathroom's mirror. He was right. Julia-Rae returned to sitting room to tell him he was right and that she was sorry. That somewhere inside while that spark of love for him still existed. Only she couldn't deal with him and what he had done right now. She needed some time to process.

Only, Roy was gone. He had left. She heard footsteps in the hallway, through the open door to the apartment. Julia-Rae ran to the door and was comforted by the site of Mrs. Leighton coming up the hallway.

"He's gone dearie. You most likely won't see him again that's one man that can vanish like the wind. It's a shame, I was hoping he'd love you enough to want to get back together."

Julia-Rae ran outside, he was nowhere to be seen. She drove to his place, if he was there he wouldn't answer the intercom and building security wouldn't let her in.

She left several messages on his voice mail in the next few days. Roy never replied. Stanza remained adamant that no such man existed. He had vanished. Angie had spoken the truth. She contacted Antonio via the cell phone number he'd left on the original papers. He texted back that Roy had quit and there was to be no deal between Stanza and The Edge.

Julia-Rae hung up the phone. The man she wanted to love had effectively disappeared off the face of the earth. The one man she was willing to set aside betrayal and want to make another attempt to be with. Dad was right, me and my temper. Only she'd learned the lesson too late.

Chapter Thirteen

Julia-Rae sat in a small patio overlooking the blue-jeweled waters of Lake Louise the next weekend. Bright red carnations and earthy yellow peonies adorned the fringes of the balcony. Already the crisp mountain air spoke of winter's eminent arrival. Julia-Rae had been enjoying her tea, its rich deep tones of Earl Grey spoke to her of proper British upbringing. Her grandma often drank tea and even as a child Julia-Rae would share the ritual of an afternoon tea. Of course there were always tea biscuits and rich butter tarts to be had at every proper gathering for tea, not a thing for a girl trying to keep her figure. They managed to ward off the bitter taste of tea for a sweet-toothed nine-year old. Now Julia-Rae relished the heat of the tea to warm her in the cool air. By this time next month the ground would begin to cover up in its annual white coat. It was a shame that her grandma wasn't alive now to talk to her and consul her, Julia-Rae sighed. The patio door to the balcony slid open.

"It's a wonder we haven't had snow yet, probably one of those El Nino things, I'm sure. How you doing, girlfriend?" Linda said as she entered the airy space of the balcony. "I didn't bother to knock on your door, I'm late as usual."

"Oh that's okay. I know you're working. Help yourself to some tea while it's still warm. Doesn't take long to begin cooling off in this part of the world. Actually I was enjoying the peace and quiet. It's funny I'd come here to escape from Roy. You know I was pretty leery coming here when I talked to you. I mean this is the first place we nearly made love. I really thought I'd be angry at the memories here."

"But you're not?" Linda sat beside Julia-Rae on the wrought iron chair. Its coolness sent shivers through her. She poured herself a tea.

“No, actually, I feel sad inside, more then anything else. Sad, and at the same time a certain sense of peace.”

“That’s great Julia-Rae that means you are beginning to let go and the sooner you do the better. You need to get on with the rest of your life.”

“How’s the rancher friend you met last week, what’s his name?”

“Jake, Jake Holden. Well, he turned out to be a little more than a rancher.”

Julia-Rae knew Linda’s ‘Well’ statement was the leading to a very interesting story. Every time she used that same tone of voice, in their college days, it meant there was an interesting story about to unfold.

“Remember I told you that he told me he had a small ranch spread down on the edge of the prairie. It was small, all right, small compared to the other ranches around it. Still five hundred head of cattle and a couple thousand acres of land is nothing to sneeze about. I'm not sure how many ranch hands work for him, but it's a few."

"Wow, pretty big operation."

"Yeah, it was an interesting couple of weeks." She smiled with that wistful smirk Julia-Rae had seen many times before, clouding her eyes. Linda in wonder-lust again.

It so reminded her of the look she had herself when her and Roy were here the last time. It was that same look she still had reverberating inside of her. The look that she hadn't been able to shake since she last talked to Roy. She hadn't spoke or heard his voice since their last meeting at Mrs. Leighton's place. The meeting that old gal had set up trying to get the two of them back together. It had been a month, she still called to leave a message to call him back nearly every day. She still recalled the hurt in his eyes. The tears that flowed long and hard behind the wheel of her car. To have a man like him walk out and not get a chance to respond. Yet, every time she picked up that telephone her integrity smacked her across the face. He lied to you lady, he wanted to screw you out of your business, your life's work. That's all he really only wanted of you. Julia-Rae struggled to keep the tears from flowing down her cheeks. Someday maybe she'd believe that lie, someday.

"But I'm not going to get into the details, maybe another day, suffice to say he wants to see me again. Right now I just want to hear how you're doing, you told me it was all over between you two. Tell me what you're feeling Julia-Rae. It helps to talk it out with a friend, you know." Linda reached over and held Julia-Rae's hand.

"I don't know Linda. Does breaking up always hurt this bad? The pain it's like a jagged knife being stabbed right into my heart and hot fire searing at my soul. I thought I could get over him eventually. But every time I hear his name or someone mentions something that reminds me of him, I want to break down and cry." Her hand shook as Linda held it. “Yet my integrity keeps saying no, damn it, no. He used me.”

“You two did make love, correct.”

“Yes, it was incredible.”

“Something I learned long ago, from some courses I took on spirituality and the human soul.”

Julia-Rae remembered when Linda took those courses, it was about three years ago. She accepted a position working here right after that and seemed a lot more together and happier.

“We are all composed of some kind of energy inside of us and there is energy flowing in and out of us all the time. This energy can also get tied up in a person or around events, usually from our past and sometimes drain us.”

Julia-Rae thought about what Linda had said, it was true she did feel totally drained. “That is exactly how I’m feeling, each step, each breath even, seems so hard and heavy.”

“That is because you two were sharing energy when you’re in love, and that is very uplifting, now the source is gone and instead of building energy and creating a new joined soul between the two of you, he’s not here. His ties that are linked to you are now leaching energy away from you. Trust me girl you are being drained and will be until you get him out of your system.”

“Is that what people mean when they say they are carrying around baggage from the past?”

“Yes, exactly. Now every time you make love with someone you establish a psychic bond between your souls, especially when two people really love each other.”

Julia-Rae thought of her dad and mom. “Is that why when one person dies in a long term relationship the other usually does shortly after?”

“Yes, partly, often in older couples, when one dies the other does very soon after. It’s like having half of your soul ripped out of you. There are so many psychic bonds established it's just like the two souls have become one. The term soulmates is truer then most people realize. Obviously you really trusted him and let him into your heart and the two of you created some pretty deep bonds. "

"But we only made love once!" Julia-Rae thought about her dad, now she understood how he felt after her mom died.

"Once is enough, especially if his feelings for you run as deep as yours for him. His psychic bond to you is very strong. So tell me what happened after you found out the truth about him."

Julia-Rae took a sip of the now cooled tea and began. The words Linda spoke she had a hard time believing yet she also trusted her best friend's judgment and wisdom.

"You mean after all that he quit his company and gave up everything."

"Yes, for me, he says."

"I think he speaks the truth and loves you deeply."

"But he lied to me, deceived me. Linda, he went to bed with me just to take away my company. Screwed me for a lousy business move."

"Yeah, that's true and in the end, he fell in love with you and gave up everything he had to want to be with you."

"I think his guilt got to him." Julia-Rae stopped and stared out at the mountains. A tear streamed down her face; she didn't want to get into blaming him. "I guess the truth is I just can't let go of him and I realize I need to in order to get with my life."

"Now listen, this is very important. Can you forgive him?

Forgiveness is mandatory in order for you to move on."

"Forgive him? For what he did to me."

"Yes, forgive him. Now I didn't say you had to like him or want to be with him, just forgive him. Otherwise, you're tying up energy in the past and carrying the baggage of it with you, dragging you down in anything you do in the present. And the longer you go dragging it along the harder and more energy you tie into him."

"Think so?" Somehow, she knew as crazy as it sounded Linda was speaking the truth. "Linda I'll try anything in order to get him out of my life and heart."

"Good, now after you forgive him you need to sever the psychic bonds established between the two of you."

"Sever!" The word sent a chill through her. She didn't like the sound of that word and everything it implied.

"Yes sever, you sever psychic bonds with psychic scissors and the best place to do this is a place where you have the most energy tied up regarding him."

"And where is that, I'm not going back to his condo?"

"No, I was thinking more along the lines of that mountain hike you two took. There's lots of unfinished business there and that is where some of the fireworks between you two began." Linda quickly explained to Julia-

Rae how to go into a relaxed state and perform the visualization needed to cut Roy's psychic bonds that were attached to her soul.

Julia-Rae's heart rose up through her throat as Linda spoke. Did part of her really want Roy out of her life? From inside the truth came bleating at her on silent wings. Did she or could she ever trust him again. She knew what the truth was, Julia-Rae also knew she had to get him out of her life, so she could get on living her life, without him.

Whatever it took, even something that sounded a little bit bizarre and off the wall as using psychic scissors to cut his hold on her heart. She would try anything to get rid of him and Julia-Rae trusted Linda, she'd been friends for many years. There was only one little part of this idea of Linda's she didn't like. "You mean up there, alone on the trail. Aren't there mountain lions and bears running around out there? I mean this is a national park."

“No at this time of the year most of the bears have already begun hibernation mode and after all that trail is well used. Wild animals usually keep away from the trails.”

“Are you sure?” While she had gone off taking pictures in some fairly inaccessible regions, Julia-Rae had never gone off wondering alone in a park where the humans were intruding on the animals. They have more rights here then we do, she thought.

Linda glanced at her watch. “Look, I got to get back to work. How about we get back together tonight when I’m off duty around 7:00? I could go with you then, if you want.” Linda said as she rose, sipped at the last of her now cold tea. “And hey, don’t forget something above all else, be kind to yourself. Oh and trust me you’ll feel incredible after this is all over and you’ve got all this released energy. Let me know, alone is better, but I’m here for you.”

Julia-Rae rose and gathered up her teapot and cup and re-entered the hotel room. The memory of last time she was here with Roy.

Him pressing her against the door to her room. The strong, musky odor of him, the crispness of his shaving cream. The hardness of his body and of his maleness as he held her against the door from behind. His want, hot and sensuous, breathing down on the back of her neck. The moisture of his lips caressing the fine hairs on the nape of her neck. Julia-Rae entered the bathroom and stared into the mirror. "How do you get rid of something that more then anything else I wanted to have? I always believed a man would enter my life, the man I've always wanted and I got to let him go." A sigh escaped her lips as she turned and opened the gold edged shower stall door. Its knurled glass face no longer held any reflection. The water hissed as she turned the tap, sending a curling cloud of mist into the air. Julia-Rae stripped and entered the security of the shower. As she leaned her head back, she let the heat of the water stream down her back washing away last nights sleep. Washing away Roy and all that could have been. She knew what she had to do.

Julia-Rae walked across the little bridge that separated the general parking lot from the hotel, for the third time. Beneath the cold silt laden waters of Lake Louise flowed quietly on their way to the sea. Someone dressed in a hotel uniform walked by. “Excuse me could you tell me where the trailhead to the Fairview Lookout trail is?” She’d been walking around in circles for the last few minutes, unable to find the trailhead. Maybe she should wait for Linda after all. No, damnit woman grab your vagina and get up that mountainside or you don’t deserve to be called Julia-Rae McNaughton.

“Yes, it’s just behind the Bear Warning sign by the old park Ranger cabin, just go up the trail at the end of the parking lot, can’t miss it.”

“Thanks.” She didn’t recall the bear sign last time. But then all she could really think about was Roy back then and why she couldn’t remember where the trail started. The bright red background and the menacing grizzly bear did little to calm down her nerves as she reached the sign. “Think positive girl, you have to do this in order to move on.” There were still quite a few cars in the parking lot and that meant undoubtedly there were a few people on the trail. “It’ll be okay,” she reassured herself slinging her canteen over her shoulder. Julia-Rae bent over and retied her hiking shoes. A familiar sound of incessant clicking from a camera’s shutter shattered the serenity of the mountain air. “Roy?” She gasped as she turned around. Her heart quit beating, “please don’t be here,” she whispered. A man stood just a few feet from her snapping pictures of the old cabin and of the emerald blue waters of the lake. He was too short and fat to be Roy. Just another tourist obviously overcome with the grandeur of Lake Louise and its environs.

Julia-Rae turned and began her hike, her hike to forget Roy. The clicking of the camera faded into the background, as the pine trees fell in all around her and she started the uphill slog to reach the meadow. Linda was right, as this incident just showed her. Roy definitely drew too much energy from her. She had to get rid of him, in order to move on in her life. How do you cleanse from your system the man you love? Each step drew her further from the safety of civilization and further into the depths of the forest until all she could hear was the raggedness of her breathing and the rustle of pine trees. Linda had better be right about this as the forest closed itself around her.

As she hiked Julia-Rae could feel her nerves calming down as she settled into the rhythm of the hike. Finally, after an hour of hiking she reached the meadow. Lilliputian flowers and short grasses greeted her as she slumped into the cool comfort of the alpine environment. It wasn't hard to find the very spot of their picnic. The meadow still bore bent grasses and crushed alpine flowers, just like it had been yesterday. She had read somewhere that it took nearly twenty years for some flowers to bloom this high up on the mountain. So short was the growing season. She believed it now. Already hints of snow had nestled in deeper pockets of refuge from the sun. It wouldn't be long and winter would obliterate all with its smothering coat and frigid breath. Air that she imagined, still smelt of passion and desire. Air where she had first begun to fall in love with the stranger called Roy Sutter. Julia-Rae took a sip from her canteen as she tried to relax. Each painful step on the way up here had reminded her of Roy. Things they'd talked about, brief stops they'd taken to admire the scenery or the plant life. The tautness of his muscles, in his legs, as he walked in front of her. The mix of his masculine sweat and graceful earthiness. But most of all she remembered his eyes. So full of serenity and the passion of life, like the tropical waters surrounding some pacific island shore. Eyes of powdered blue chalk mixed with the rich seductive tones of his voice.

Julia-Rae breathed in a deep breath, pulling in her stomach and breathing from her diaphragm. Erase it all, blank your mind, she told herself. Keep breathing deep from the diaphragm, Linda said, letting your mind blank. Relax yourself and eventually tune out your thoughts and become one. One with yourself and one with the nature in you. She thought Linda was cracked and yet as she continued to take in deep slow relaxing breaths, Julia-Rae could feel the peace begin to enter herself. Linda said she'd do this every weekend, just sit still and drop all the machinations of her hectic life and meditate for half an hour or so. Each breath, deep and rich, washed away the tension and pressure of her life back in Edmonton. Here there was only her and this mountain. She couldn't remember the last time she had just sat still and let herself be at peace. The coolness of the mountain air washed over her, filling her with the quiet solidity of the mountain. Each breath diluted herself until she could feel the heaven and earth flowing in her and all around her. It was an incredible experience, one Linda called, becoming one with nature. Simply reconnecting with the world to which we all came from, she said. Julia-Rae made a mental note to do with on a regular basis.

Julia-Rae simply enjoyed the swish of the summer breeze as it stirred the limbs of the pines and played in the grass. Then she began to imagine a white light streaming down over her, filling her with energy. Bathing her in its pure essence. Julia-Rae allowed herself to be lifted from her body. Until she could look down at herself sitting cross-legged on the meadow. Until all she could see was just the pure energy of who she was, her soul, as Linda had called it. Then she concentrated on pulling up a mental picture of Roy. The pure white self of Roy, his soul. The very core of the man. The man she had allowed herself to truly love. The image of both of them began to waver as her emotions sprang alive, the pangs of love and the hurt of betrayal. No keep focus, girl, she thought. Emotions are needed, but don't swim in them or she'll lose the whole picture she was trying to create.

Julia-Rae focused again on the figures of their souls. In the space between the two she saw the lines forming. The thin tendrils of psychic energy that attached the two, connecting them. Her emotions, her heart, her love, all were there, inexorably wove to this man, Roy Sutter. All the links between them stood revealed. Julia-Rae took a deep breath and pulled from her mind a pair of gleaming, silver scissors. From each band of energy, she could feel the drain. Siphoning off who she was, sucking her vital life force into trying to combine the two separate hearts into one heart. Trying to become soulmates, as Linda had said. It was all so clear now.

Slowly she placed one of the throbbing bonds between the sharp edges of the opened scissors and slowly cut into the bond. With a snap, a twinge of pain and of remorse, the link between them fell away. That severed half hung there and she concentrated on pulling it back within herself. As she did Julia-Rae felt her energy increase, her freedom and the love for herself. Then she cut another and another link, each becoming easier to sever then the last as she felt less and less of the ties between Roy and her. Until a single bond remained between her and Roy. Between her and what once was and what could have been. From deep within came bubbling the emotion of regret, of pain. Knowing she would sever all that could have been, the love she had, strong and intense, for this man. The joy, the future they might have possessed. All ending, each breath she drew in sent all of that withering away as her soul gained its strength again. As Roy faded away into the past.

There was still one strand remaining. This she had to do and as Julia-drew in a deep breath, she knew she had the strength now.

The snap of a twig startled her. Damn, probably someone coming up the trail. Jarred from her concentration the images began to dissipate. "Okay girl, pull yourself back into your work."

She shut out the movement coming up the trail. One bond left to cut, don't let anything distract me from that now. She knew that once she cut that last bond she'd be able to face Roy again and move on with her life. Get over him, forget him. The shimmer of the scissors pulled everything back into place. Pulled taunt by the tug of the two souls, all the love she possessed for Roy, flowed through this last link. The two souls tried to pull apart and begin their own lives. Changing, each in their own way she knew, until there would no longer any attraction or link between the two. They had crossed paths at this moment and would never again. Slowly she parted the jaws of the scissors and placed that one last strand between them. A deep breath of courage and she began to close the scissors on the past, on Roy.

A deep growl rent the serene stillness of the mountainside, tearing the visions before her away, pulling Julia-Rae back to the security of her body and her surroundings.

Back to the fact that she was alone, utterly alone, on this trail. Kilometers from known civilization and help, alone with whatever was lumbering towards her on the trail.

Chapter Fourteen

Roy sped up the trail. Something beat an ugly message into his heart. “Fool woman hiking alone on a trail in the mountains, especially that one.” He knew grizzly’s haunted alpine meadows. And while normally they wouldn’t be on that trail with the number of hikers normally around, this late in the year they tend to come down off the higher elevations in search of food before winter sets in. And there probably weren’t many other hikers on that trail in late September. “Damn!” he had a bad feeling in the pit of his guts. Especially with that bear warning sign at the foot of the trail, Roy redoubled his efforts climbing up the trail.

Another growl, closer, more menacing. Something heavy moving in her direction.

Fear slammed its fist into her. Gunshot adrenaline sent Julia-Rae reeling to her feet. How horrifying to realize in a freakish instant that you are alone on a mountain trail, Julia-Rae thought. She felt so helpless and weak as the image of a bear shambled towards her. Terror seared into her catatonic mind. Run, she had to run. Her feet, purged of any will power, refused to move.

Would a woman of adventure let herself be overcome by an approaching bear? No, she'd use her head, Julia-Rae thought. Her whole body began shaking form the adrenaline flooding her system. "Move damn it, move." Slowly, she began to step backwards and that was a mistake. Julia-Rae realized all too late as her memory flooded back from its brief hiatus of induced terror. Hadn't she read that bears have dismal eyesight and exceptional smell? Well, it might not have already smelt her, but now it sure did see her. The bear roared in defiance as Julia-Rae tried to turn in an attempt to run.

Its voice rooted her to the ground, sucking any semblance of will power from her. She stood there as bear rose onto its hind legs. It roared again as it advanced.

She was going to die, here, alone on this mountain. Here and now. Life wasn't supposed to end like this. What to do? If only Roy was. . .

"Put your head down and slump your shoulders forward, now." Growled a familiar voice from behind her. Stunned, she turned her head trying to catch a glimpse of the familiar voice.

"To that bear you're challenging his territory by standing upright. Cower, damn it. And if I yell drop. Drop like a rock, lay very still and put your hands over your head protecting the back of your head and face."

"What?" How dare he talk to her like that? The bear let out a loud bellow.

"Cower, head down, slump your shoulders forward. Now damn it. Otherwise he thinks you are challenging him.

Don't turn your back to him, face him and do as I say, otherwise I'll have to tackle it myself."

Julia-Rae did as Roy said. The bear slowed its advance.

"I know what I'm talking about, the longer you stand there and challenge him the angrier he gets. That's a grizzly and they have hair thin tempers. Now move backwards, head down. I didn't come up here looking for you to lose you to a bear. Very slowly back up towards me. It's a signal that you are conceding his territory to him. He is the dominate one." She jerked her leg backwards, wanting to run. It shook so bad she thought it would fall off.

"Focus on the ground, don't make eye contact with him and keep coming towards me."

The bear fell to all fours as Julia-Rae kept walking backwards, Roy guiding her left or right. Each heartbeat an eternity as Roy's voice grew louder and closer.

She jumped as the warmth of his hand gripped her shoulder.

"Oh, Roy, I thought I was going to die back."

"We still might. Oh, shoot!" He responded looking over her shoulder. "He's coming this way. They have great sense of smell, do you have any food in that backpack."

"Just a couple of chocolate bars, some water and a couple of apples, why."

Roy tore the backpack from her shoulders and began rummaging through her pack. "We're not out of the woods yet. He's coming this way." He pulled free the food. "Okay get running now, I'll be right behind you."

Julia-Rae wanted to stay and die beside her man. Yet she trusted him, he had come here looking for her and now was willing to put his life on the line for her. "Roy I. . ."

"Just keep backing up damn it, who knows what he might do next. Griz are so unpredictable and temperamental. We're not out of danger yet, if we make it out of this alive, we'll talk later." Roy ripped open the chocolate bars and threw them on the trail, along with the apples. He stomped on the apples; the sweet scent flooded the air. Head down, he began backing up after Julia-Rae. She watched the bear shuffle forwards until he stopped and sniffed at the chocolate bars.

Roy turned and ran to her, "Okay now, while he's distracted, run. I'll be right behind you."

How long she ran, didn't register, an eternity it seemed. Finally she turned, glancing over her shoulder and stopped. He wasn't anywhere to be seen. "Roy?" No response. "Roy!" broke from her lips again. Only the silence of the forest and its muted voices replied. He had come here to find her. He said so, he was back there on that trail, with that huge bear.

He would have risked his life to defend her, barehanded. Perhaps, it got him and he was already dead. The thought sent screams of panic through her. No, not as long as that one thread of love remained. "Roy, I'm coming." Her own safety didn't matter now, she had to know if he was still alive and if he wasn't it didn't matter if she did. Julia-Rae didn't want to continue living, not in a world without him. "Roy, please be alive." She began to walk briskly back up the trail. They met nearly head on as he sped around a large growth of trees.

"Jesus, woman, I said get running." His hands shook her, his blue eyes full of concern and worry.

"I had to know if you're still okay."

"Hey I'm here, now let's get moving before our ursine friend decides to take up the chase again. In a couple of minutes, we should be downwind from him and safe."

Roy grabbed her hand with a strong yet demanding grip and nearly pulled her off her feet as he began to run. His hand felt so good so natural holding hers. They tore down the trail together, not looking to see if the bear was coming. An insane flight through the forest, fleeing from death, holding the hand of the man she loved. Time, her feet, all were fleeting, meaningless. Julia-Rae wanted to run forever, handing his hand. Pines whizzed by, her breath caught in her throat. Caught, between wanting to cry stop and catch a breath, or keep on running. They kept on running putting as much distance between the bear and them as possible.

Finally, she couldn't run any further. "I gotta stop. Aren't we safe in the trees?" Julia-Rae gasped as she stopped and slumped over struggling to suck in as much air as possible.

"No, they can smell a rotting carcass miles away. Let's keep walking at least. You can't tell how long he's going to be distracted. When we get back down, I'll alert the park rangers, they'll close this trail for a few days and then see if the bear is still hanging around, there's a good chance he'll be getting ready to go into hibernation."

"Why can't they just shoot him and be done with it. That bear nearly had me for his lunch."

"No, Julia-Rae, the bear is just being a bear, we are after all, trespassing in his space. If he's trouble, they might have to tranquilize him and relocate him a few miles away. More than likely he'll just move on."

His words puzzled Julia-Rae. It never dawned on her that it was the humans that were the intruders. Of course there were other kinds of intruders in life. "Speaking of intruders what exactly are you doing here?"

"I called your work yesterday, they said you took off to the mountains for the weekend, I have to talk to you."

"There's no talking Roy, it is over." That one psychic thread remaining between them Julia-Rae could feel, undulating like an agitated snake unable, unwilling to let go of either end. Was it over? Why hadn't she cut that one last thread? In the green sheltered canopy of the forest he looked so handsome. She wanted to run her fingers through that short mane of golden hair he possessed, stirred into reckless abandon by their running. His breath, filled with the freshness of mountain air and his musky scent of their running, fell against her face. The hard line of his lips, flushed with color and life, that had once felt so delicious against hers, seemed to beg for a kiss.

"They told me you'd gone for a few days to the mountains. I knew you came here. So I called to check your reservation and came right down. I don't know what it was but the minute I got out of the car I could sense something was wrong. I don't know what it was, call it my gut reaction, intuition, but something wasn't right. When I got to the front desk, I met the blonde waitress, Denise that had served us that night we had supper together."

"Actually, Linda."

"Correct, except her name tag read business manager, I knew something was fishy. A hotel establishment the size of this place would never have a manager double as a waitress."

"Yes, we were trying to see how much you really liked me, Linda was trying to flaunt herself to sidetrack your attention. An old game we played from our younger college days working in this old restaurant in Edmonton." She smiled remembering the good times she and Linda had back then, remembering the look of indignation on Roy's face as Linda bent over him. She especially remembered the look in his eyes, the hunger like a wolf on the prowl. Hungry and dangerous, as he dropped her off at her door that night. More than anything she wanted him to hold her right now.

"Judging by her reaction, I knew something was wrong. She quickly told me she was an old friend and that you had gone off for a hike on the same trail we'd been on before. I knew I had to find you before it was too late." Roy stopped walking on the trail. "Didn't you see the bear warning sign at the trailhead? This time of year the bears come down off the mountain slopes and search for only one thing, food."

Julia-Rae looked down at the ground. "I guess I had eyes for only one thing back then myself."

He grabbed Julia-Rae's hand, spun her around and pressed her up against a large pine tree they had to negotiate around on the trail. He stared deep into her eyes. The thrust of her breasts brought an erotic surge through him. He remembered the first time he had pinned her up against that stone wall at Machu Picchu. The passion in her eyes, the desire, was still there. Along with that zest and fire that resided in her soul. The fire and zest he had come to love. That was what drove him to sleepless nights, since they split. Tossing and turning every night. Staring at his pictures on the wall, realizing how meaningless it all seemed without her. "Why is it every time I touch you, hold you, I feel myself slip away from reality and enter some lost world of passion. I hate being alone in my condo, the scent of your perfume I can still smell lingering in the air. The smell of you on the bed sheets. It's like having a ghost, an erotic ghost, haunting my life. I've tendered my resignation to the company, they've agreed to it and gave me a substantial severance package. Now there's only one thing in my life that's missing." The rise of her firm breasts, the heat of her body called to him. He wanted so badly to crush those red lips to his and rip her clothes from her. Claim her as his woman, his mate, to trumpet his chest like Tarzan would after having met Jane. It was all sheer insanity; his whole life had become insanity since he met her. He'd given up his career, his business, everything except the one thing that wasn't an option in his life, his son.

But first he knew he had to talk to her, make her see that he really loved her. That he, Ray Sutfield wanted this woman in his life.

The coolness of the mountain air, alive with the crisp caution of winters immanent arrival. The roughness of the pine tree, its sap filling his lungs with a cloying odor, did little to soothe his desire. The heat of her body, the softness of her breasts, crushing against him and those lips. The hunger stirred deep within and Roy answered its call.

Julia-Rae fell silent as Roy talked. She saw the passion stir as his words filled her ears and caressed her heart. The passion that rose like smoke off mysterious lake waters in the cool of the night and swirled in his eyes. She could feel her body responding to his, calling to him. Shivers ranged across her skin as his mouth descended over hers. His eyes closed and their lips touched. His cold, hard lips touching hers, kissing hers. Ray's tongue brushed the surface of her lips, lightly. A teasing snake of desire. Julia-Rae parted hers, letting him enter. Mutual moans broke quietness of the trail. She pulled back for a moment and whispered, "Tell me what you want Ray, tell me now."

His left hand encircled her waist and pulled her into his embrace.

Ray's face drew close again, his breath, hot with hunger, traced a delicate line to her ear. Barely touching the surface of her skin, just moving amongst the fine hairs of her neck like a tiger stalking its prey, excited by the hunt, licked her mouth slowly.

A moan escaped from deep within Julia-Rae, the sheer erotic arousal of his action sent a shudder through her legs to that place that needed him the most. That place of wetness that craved him. She felt the heat of his hardness, his desire for her against her, wanting her. His mouth, the mouth that had kissed and tasted all of her once before, breathed in her ear.

"It's you, I need now, since I first met you. I can't deny the truth that beats within. Since I've last seen you I've gone to bed unable to sleep. Wakeless nights, tossing and turning. Thinking of you, of holding you again, of kissing you and. . ." His voice slipped low until barely a hush, "making love to you."

As he spoke Julia-Rae felt her legs go weak and parted ever so slightly until she rested herself on his thigh. His hardness she felt throbbing, straining to be inside of her.

"You, Julia-Rae, it's you I love and have since I laid eyes on you. I realize I can't give back the trust I've broken, but-"

"Ray." She didn't want to hear his words, his reasons, she just wanted him to be inside of her.

"Yes."

"Don't say another word. Just kiss me again and don't stop. Make love to me."

"Here?"

"Yes, here. Here and now, right now. More then anything I want you. You've proven to me you love me by coming out here. I tried to break that bond between our hearts and get over my life. I'll explain later. I realized that this is not what I really want."

"What is it you really want?"

"You, I love you Roy, I can't deny myself that truth any longer, make love to me."

"What if someone comes? What if the bear comes up the trail?"

"Then I guess they'll be in for a shock, won't they and as for that bear. Didn't I hear you say you were a man of risk and adventure?"

She smiled and parted her lips. "Risk with me, dare me."

"But I didn't bring any protection."

"Roy make love to me right now and I don't want anything between feeling you inside of me. I want you, naked inside of me."

Ray pulled her against him and pressed the two of them to the hard bark of the tree. The scents of pine sap, sticking to her clothes filled the air and inflamed their senses. She didn't care, clothes be damned she only wanted Ray. Julia-Rae wanted this man, here and now. His eyes were on fire with passion, as she closed hers and felt the hunger of his lips, as they devoured hers. She put her hands around him and drew him in tight. The hardness in his jeans pressed against her, burning her with desire and Julia-Rae returned that thrust with one of hers. They began to move in that ancient dance of lovers. The slow, sensuous sway of hips, moving to the heat of the passion building between their loins. An inescapable madness of sensuous pleasures that build upon themselves. Demanding release, sweet release.

"I want to, but it's…" he tried to say as she reached down and began to stroke his hardness. He moaned uncontrollably, with his head thrown back.

"No words, we'll talk later. I want you Roy, right now, inside of me, driving me and yourself mad with desire." With that she deftly reached over with her one hand and unbuttoned his fly.

"Oh God, what you do to me."

Roy reached down and unhitched her hiking pants and getting on bended knee, he pulled her pants down and off. Julia-Rae shuddered as his rough hands caressed her legs. The delightful sensation of his hard hands, cold from the air, against her soft legs, stroking her very wetness. A finger running deep into that vee. Roy reached up and pulled down her panties. She was wet, she knew that much. This wasn't supposed to be happening. She had come up this mountain looking for release from the madness of him. Shudders ran through her as his finger dipped into her center again. Wave after wave sent her crashing into the rocks. "Oh my god, stop!" It was too intense, another couple of seconds of this and she'd be a quivering mass of incoherent pleasure. Julia-Rae pulled Ray's head away from her. "Not now, I'm too aroused, this is too intense, later my darling, right now I need to feel you."

Understanding, Ray rose and quickly unzipped his jeans. They landed in a heap beside hers. Julia-Rae opened her eyes as he stepped forward and that hardness entered her, filling her. He held her against the tree as he drove slowly inside of her. "Are you okay?" He looked concerned not knowing if her cry was of joy or pain.

"Oh yes, this is incredible." Julia-Rae flung back her tresses of red hair and pulled Ray into her arms. The roughness of the pine bark, its stickiness, the liberating fresh smells of the forest all drove into her mind. From deep down inside she could already feel the building explosion.

"Oh, I'm going to…" was all Ray had a chance to say as the surge like being shot out of a cannon overwhelmed him. Julia-Rae let out a deep moan and he knew she was exploding also. He kept stroking even as his legs lost all sensation, until the intensity became too much. "Julia-Rae, I love you, I have since I first saw you in that cloud of dust in Peru."

"Ray, I love you too, kiss me. You do things to me I've never even dreamt of experiencing, let alone doing."

"I don't know where to begin." He fell against her, limp.

"Why don't we begin by getting our clothes on and going back up to my room?"

Her back was raw, she'd be bruised for days, yet she didn't care. The smell of earth and pine sap clung to her. "We could get cleaned up and talk and this time take our pleasure out a little slower."

"Now that lady, is a great idea, I like how you think." He kissed her softly, gently.

When they got back to her room, Julia-Rae called up Linda. "Hey, remember that idea we had about filling a bathtub full of Jell-o?"

"Yes I sure do, a little sticky but wouldn't it be a blast to make love in."

"Think you could arrange it for tonight? Great, and make it red Jell-o."

Epilogue

The next month they got married. The next issue of New Edge for Modern Couples had on its cover the picture of Carrie from Roy's pictures, suspended in the fog on the escarpment of rock jutting out from the side of the mountain. It was Julia-Rae's idea, a kind of tribute to the adventuresome spirit in all women. That they need to be true to themselves in order to attract the man that would be the same into their hearts and lives. They worked together producing the magazine, going on crazy assignments into remote parts of the world. Nine months later, the picture of Sean wrapped in swaddling clothes on the cover, announced the arrival of their new daughter, Chelen Sutfield, another fiery redhead to the world.

Sean came to live with them, Julia-Rae wouldn't have it any other way. They talked Mrs. Leighton into joining the nursing home, only under the condition that Ray come and read her and Helene passages from romance novels. “And read us again those hot juicy parts in your deep low sexy voice,” they’d say in unison, like the two little giddy girls they really were at heart.

And Above All Else

To my wife Jenny; who does all of my corrections, grammar and proper punctuation before the rest of the world, and any editor, gets to see it, along with putting up with all of my sh*t. This novel and all of my others wouldn't be possible without all of her work.

PS. And she still loves me unconditionally (also she just edited this over my shoulder!).

If you really enjoyed this novel,

please feel free to leave a review.

The author will highly appreciate it

And will help my rankings on Amazon

Thank You!

Novels Under the Pseudonym
Felicity Talisman

Two heart-wrenching tragedies in the same week served as a stark reminder of the brevity of life. It was time for Leanne to free herself from the humdrum world of real estate and fulfill her heart's desire. The need to achieve her dream became even more poignant when she discovered her mother had carried the same dream of wanting to paint, but self-doubt had prevented her from even trying.

Leanne embarked on a road-trip to Banff, a town nestled in the heart of the magnificent Rocky Mountains, surrounded by the most perfect of nature's beauty. Since this was where her parents had fallen in love, it felt crucial to achieve their shared dream there. However, unbeknownst to Leanne, her run-of-the-mill road-trip turns into anything but and her journey to fulfillment becomes even stranger than fiction.

Shuttered Seductions Romance Novel

She only wanted Not to fall in love with him.

He only wanted to steal her company. Roy only wanted to seduce Julia-Rae and convince her to sell him her company. Julia-Rae wanted to shut him out of her heart like every other man that ever got close. Only what do you do when you fall in madly in love with the enemy and the enemy with you. Will the dark secrets they hold tear them apart or bring them closer together?

Autumn's Summer

Written in his wife's hand a beautiful leather-bound diary is delivered a year after her passing which contains many secrets. Showing how his lonely empty-nester wife's life changed profoundly after a purely-by-chance meeting in, of all places, a mundane, corner grocery store. She embarks on a voyage of discovery with the spiritualist, Summer, to find new meaning to her life, that, once commenced, transports her to realms and dimensions she never knew existed.

A contemporary literary romance novel mixed with a suspense-filled mystery thriller. The writer combines magical realism and paranormal urban fantasy on a profoundly spiritual level unlike any novel you have ever, or will ever, read.

Reviews

I thought I'd have a quick peek at Autumn's Summer and then finish the book I was currently reading! I was entranced and spellbound from that moment, my current read neglected! Couldn't put it down, read it in one day. Yes, the love scenes were intense, passion blossoms in many forms! I enjoyed this immensely!

Shelley W.

Run, don't walk to your nearest bookseller and pick up a copy of Felicity Talisman's Autumn's Summer. I didn't know what to expect from the book, but I was immediately drawn into the world the author has created. It has everything a reader could want, real characters in a fantasy world while bridging the gap between fantasy and reality.

Great job by this Canadian author!

Greenhill

***5.0 out of 5 stars* Five Star Review**

"Autumn's Summer" is very complex, and readers will begin to develop feelings for the characters as if they were real people you could become friends with. Each character is multi-faceted, and the storyline is completely believable. The intertwining of Celtic beliefs and legends throughout the story offers readers a wonderful way to get to know Celtic history while reading along. The author even offered an additional section called Celtic Facts, Legends and History if you are so inclined to want to learn more about Celtic history and practices.

Overall, "Autumn's Summer" by Felicity Talisman is rich in details, especially in Celtic legends and traditions. The characters will enchant you and the story will entertain any reader who appreciates great characters. It's well worth looking into!

Life had seemed to be unfulfilled for Autumn for quite a few years, but she never completely realized it until she saw an ad in the local grocery store for someone offering yoga classes, meditations, and spiritual readings in "Autumn's Summer" by Felicity Talisman. Something about this ad offered by a woman named Summer caught her eye and intrigued her. While reading the ad, someone off in the near distance began watching Autumn without her knowing it. Summer just so happened to be in the store at the same time and couldn't help but approach Autumn. Both women felt a stirring inside themselves but didn't quite know what fate had in store for the both of them. They became fast friends, and this led to them having an affair together even though Autumn was married to Richard.

A fun fact explained in the back of the book is that the author's name, Felicity Talisman, is a collaboration between Frank and

his wife, Jenny Talaber. How wonderful to learn that a husband and wife team worked on creating such an entertaining story!
Reviewed by Diana Coyle for Reader Views

Afterword

Writing As Felicity Talisman

He was once told by a woman that most guys don't know how to romance let alone write it. Hence the pseudonym 'Felicity Talisman' in his more romantic ventures.

Frank's Bio

Born on the wild Canadian prairies but tired of the winter months in Edmonton, Frank immigrated to the more temperate cedar forests of coastal British Columbia. Yes, they get snow in Chilliwack during the winter months, and on that odd occasion Frank is forced to search out the snow shovel, dust off the cobwebs and have a go. At the snow, not the cobwebs.

His run-of-the-mill day job of auto technician/service advisor seems at odds with being an inspired, off-the-wall, author, but his zest for life, the environment, and the little muses that won't let his pencil stay still, spring from his mother's Hungarian ancestry. It's the Gypsy blood, he says, which pounds through his veins with wild abandon, driving him to the realms of fantasy.
This is the muse inside, the essence of Frank Talaber.

People who have read Frank's books describe him as a natural storyteller who writes like his soul is on fire and his pencil is his voice. They go further to say that they find his books grabbingly intense and hilarious at times, screaming everyday life from such a realistic viewpoint you're drawn into his world, hook, line and plum bob, unable to stop; almost cursing that they can't set the book down, page after page. Frank takes great pride in the realism of his work, painstakingly visiting most of the locations, (obviously, only the "real-life" ones!) and he is so thorough that many readers have remarked that they can hear, taste, visualize, smell and feel the essence of the place. "It really is like being there" one remarked. There isn't a greater compliment to be made.

His tagline is Canada's Foremost Off-beat Author (also the name of his YouTube channel; check it out for his witty and informative videos) who writes in urban fantasy, science fiction, crime, spiritual, romance, erotica and comedy genres. Well, anything that comes to him, basically! Except westerns. Although he does like to ride Gangnam style; does that count?

Literature written almost beyond genres, whose compelling thoughts are freed from the depths of the heart and subconscious before being poured onto the page. Or, as he often says, "you don't have to be mad to be a writer, but it sure helps".

Other Novels by Frank Talaber

***Stillwater Runs Deep* Series**

Book One: Raven's Lament

(based on a true incident)

A madman cuts down a rare tree in protest of logging, releasing something he didn't intend to. Reporter Brooke Grant investigates the story, finds the love of his life, only to lose her to said being. Enlisting the aid of a deranged shaman he has to save his love and stop the world from being changed forever.

Reviews

WHISTLER INDEPENDENT BOOK AWARDS Fiction Evaluation 2023

Easy to follow and immerse oneself into this well-told story. The pace unfolds so naturally, I forgot that I was reading - which is essential to achieving this result. Loved the narrative voice that brought Characters to life through vivid descriptions and unforced dialogue. Time and place are masterfully captured through poetic and beautiful imagery. The writing style is wonderful, a celebration of words, both visual and imaginative. This story has depth, the themes are heartfelt and lingered long after I finished reading it. The pulse of energy - otherworldly, Raven's Lament is a classic in waiting with dream-like narration. I loved every inch of it.

[Thanks Frank & good luck!] Molly Harrison WiBA Coordination

I was touched when I sensed the author's profound reverence for trees; especially when I read his descriptions of the 'sobbing trees' as they were axed down. This novel has the ring of an epic "Lord of the Rings" journey -this is one journey that I'll always remember!

This is one of these books that you don't want to lay down until it's finished. Great stuff!

Stephanie A. Bridgeman

"After being stranded twenty kilometers from the nearest road at the tip of Rose Spit, Haida Gwaii, and having to push Frank's spanking new SUV a few kilometers along the beach before the tide came in and we ran out of booze, my first reaction on being asked to write a back cover blurb was, "over my dead body." Some people will do anything to get an endorsement."

Susan Musgrave/Cargo of Orchids/Given

On The west Coast, a journalist investigates a killing linked to destruction of old growth forest on First Nations land, and finds a spirit war as well as a real-work environmental struggle. He also finds love and meaning. It's a lovely, timely story line, and the outcome is arrived at in a surprising confluence of plot and subplot which makes the book ultimately charming and moving.

Candas Jane Dorsey

Stillwater Runs Deep

Book Two: The Lure

Ever go out drinking and don't remember what you did? What if there was a bar where spirits use your body for whatever they want until you sober up? What if the city's mayor has been murdered, his family missing, no clues and a witch has been released from her centuries old imprisonment? A deranged shaman shows up leaving clues and vanishes. So begins police detective, Carol Ainsworth's first big detective case.

Here is the film pitch to the novel. I've had a request to do a possible Netflix film on this novel.

(Turn up the volume.) From My YouTube Channel, Let's Be Frank, Canada's Foremost OffBeat Author.

https://youtu.be/pa_-l2WejjA

Reviews

Your book kept my attention riveted from beginning to end. I liked the way you presented the female character being in control of the outcome and the fact the story was based on local settings. i.e. Victoria, B.C. Canada. Riveting Work .....

Linda Low

A refreshing change from the usual and all too familiar cast of deities and spirits. Talaber pulls his characters from the vast and untapped riches of aboriginal myth and legend, bringing to life their intricate stories largely unfamiliar to wider audiences. He intertwines their ancient tales with the dark, gritty and dangerous under belly of contemporary urban life. The whole makes for an interesting and compelling read with an ending that's impossible to predict.

Robert Winslow

Damn Frank -- this writing is as tactile as a 1955 T-Bird. Very nice descriptions, good dialogue, a thinking man's book but one that can be read entirely for pleasure. Good work.

Michael Arkin/Judicial Indiscretion

Paranormal fantasy, mystery thriller rolled into one. The Lure is a well-crafted story that builds suspense through flowing narrative, life-like characters, and believable dialogue. If you're a fan of any of the above mentioned genres, or if you're just looking for a page turner to get lost in, The Lure will not disappoint.

Cris Pasqueralle/Destiny Revealed

A gritty book flavored with primitive urges and mysticism. As I followed Carol's foray into the realm of shamanism, I realized that it took a special touch to pull off a complicated plot the way you did. Your prose was concise, powerfully descriptive, the dialogue lively, and your photographic mastery of the fixtures and streets in Vancouver's hub, in clear evidence.

Kenneth Edward Lim/The North Korean

Carol, the head detective, has to solve several murder cases: with many twists and turns. There's Shamans, Animal Spirits, and "The Lure" thrown in for good measure. No wonder, Carol wanted to resign! Yes, this novel is a roller-coaster ride, with the author cleverly hinting along the way, ending with a roller coaster ride! Read this book. It is different. It's as if Elmore Leonard has risen as a shaman, to guide others to write about Indian lore.

Nancy Bridgeman

Your book was a rollercoaster ride thorough my emotions which, when I got off, left me stunned and breathless.

Your portrayal of sociopaths and the criminal mind in the pursuit of the sexually willing was so disturbing I had nightmares and had to set the novel aside for days. But the writing was so compelling I had to finish it, and I'm glad I persevered.

I literally cheered "go get them!" when Charlie used his protectors to deal rather uniquely with the antagonists.

I was enlightened to the Native spiritual culture which pleased me for which I now have a greater understanding and respect.

Carol G.

I want the author to take me to their world. I love the adrenaline rush I get from reading a book that scares the crap out of me. You know, the ones that have you screaming to the characters in your head or out loud. It tells me that the author did his or her job by getting me emotionally involved. I give up on books if I don't feel something. This book isn't one of those.

April Wolfgong

Stillwater Runs Deep,

Book Three: The Awakening

Its Ghostbusters teamed up with a female Mickey Spillane who has a Native Shaman sidekick nuttier than a squirrels winter stash as a side kick.

Agatha Christie, roll over in your grave, new sleuths on the prowl. A deranged shaman breaks his way into jail to stop all hell from breaking free while police detective Carol Ainsworth has to bring justice to a forest being's murdered mother.

How angry would a mythical god be if he found himself beginning to awake inside a mortal after centuries? The duo are determined to find out who killed the previous native elder before all lightning and thunder breaks loose. They encounter deranged inmates, mystical beings, ancient serpents, wood sprites and someone who should have been dead long ago.

Not your usual crime/mystery!
Not your usual criminal investigators!
You thought Jack Nicholson was mad in The Shining…
Wait until you meet Charlie Stillwaters in the Sweat lodge.

Reviews

There are many aspects true to First Nation's beliefs. For example the transformation of animals and anomalies within our realm. Frank Talaber's writing is clear and concise, leaving no grey areas. But his true talent as a writer is not only a sense of time, history and capturing First Nation's humor, but going from the real to the surreal and the supernatural. A gift he plies very well.

Tom Patterson Nuu-Cha-Nulth Artist and Master Carver

I've read and reread his previous series, Stillwaters Run Deep, several times. Frank's writing is original and compelling. You run into characters and situations totally unexpected. Keeps you on the edge of your seat and your heart.

Greta Olsson

Just when I was beginning to wonder where the next great Canadian story teller would emerge from, Frank Talaber has written a modern crime mystery with a twist. In "The Awakening" Talaber weaves the richness of Canada's west coast aboriginal spirituality into the science of modern forensics. CSI comes to Haida Gwaii as the shaman and the detective conduct an investigation that will take them and the reader on a journey to a place where murder, redemption and ancient mysticism intersect.

Michael G. de Jong, QC, Minister of Finance, Government House Leader,

Province of British Columbia

The Ainsworth Chronicles, Book One: The Joining

Welcome to Victoria in Beautiful British Columbia, the most haunted city in North America, and to Detective Carol Ainsworth's first day undercover at the very grand old lady, The Fairmont Empress Hotel. Ready to deal with the two Italian families flying in for a wedding to unite them, she did not bargain for the ghosts, the FBI agent or the ancient curses that come along too. Add to that the very wonderful and mysterious psychic lady claiming you've invited her, the young boys disappearing, and the weird things happening to the unfortunates looking for their next fix trapped alongside spirits in the sewers, Carol found her first undercover assignment way more challenging than she could have imagined.

The one saving grace was the great Empress High Tea that Agnes introduced her to and the fabulous scones that are to die for. Literally.

Reviews

I hate you! My wife, who is off on medical leave, won't get out of the bathroom. Can't put your book down. LOL.

Bruce W.

The ghosts of Victoria, BC are restless. The Joining is a riveting read for crime fiction lovers and those fascinated by tales of hauntings. Talaber expertly draws you into a multi-leveled world of local history, crime, and the supernatural, where a blue fairy, comprised of two sorrowful creatures, is more powerful than it knows. A perfect read for those foggy West Coast nights.

Melanie Cossey, A Peculiar Curiosity

I bought four of his novels, all right up my alley, urban Fantasy and Paranormal thrillers. But as we were leaving my girlfriend opened up the copy of The Joining, I had purchased and said, "Stop! You gotta go back I have to buy this book." Frank had hooked her in the first three pages. Well Done.

Joyce Nicholls

I've read and reread his previous series, Stillwaters Run Deep, several times. Frank's writing is original and compelling. You run into characters and situations totally unexpected. Keeps you on the edge of your seat and your heart.

Greta Olsson

The Ainsworth Chronicles, Book Two: The Mystery of Ms. Teak

Agnes at her craziest best. Only what secret does she have to hide from herself and the one she thought dead? How does one psychic stop another from hunting her down, especially when the other hires the services of a mystical being long thought perished! As for Carol, she has her hands full with pissed-off Russians, the reborn builder of much of Victorian Victoria (yes, *the* Sir Francis Rattenbury), a young girl claiming to be our aforementioned psychic, and, to top it all off, there's something very wrong with Nathan, her nephew that they saved from death. But in traditional English fashion High Tea is *of course* still being served.

Reviews

I hate you, I can't put this book down. Every page gets more interesting, suspicious, wondering what is going to happen next. I sit down to only read one more chapter but end up having to read two more, because I need to know what happened in the past. Each chapter keeps you wanting more and now I hate it even more since I can’t get to it before Long weekend coming up. I just read the last six chapters, clinging to every word, every sentence thinking I know what is going to happen next. Oh no, you take me in a completely different direction. Great book.
Sandy Strebe

Fasten your seatbelt as Frank Talaber takes you on a multi-dimensional trek through time where history comes alive to reveal buried secrets and tortured souls. From the stately tea salons of old Victoria to the haunting desolation of British Columbia's rugged West coast waters, The Mystery of Ms. Teak will both entertain and invite you to confront the demons that live within us all.
Michael de Jong
Provincial BC Liberal Minister

The Mystery of Ms. Teak
Do not read this book! Seriously, do not read this book - unless you are prepared to deal with a rift on your personal timeline. You will find that this book

causes you to postpone activities that you would otherwise be doing.
You will be transported into a world of history and mystery, crime and grime, Spirits and other worldly time travel, with the delectable Detective Carol Ainsworth.
An amazing tale, which I thoroughly enjoyed.
Paddy Kopieczek

As a weaver of books you're beyond compare.
Greta Olsson

If you are into Videos, check out my newest Youtube video.
Trying To De Mystify The Mystery of Ms. Teak
https://youtu.be/TQKXOrJlpgw

On my YouTube Channel
Let's Be Frank, Canada's Foremost Off-Beat Author

Seeds Of Ascension Book One: Spirits Awakening

In a normal relationship a man gets married and has the time of his life on a memorable honeymoon in Hawaii. A small dilemma begins for Roger Harrison when normality ceases existing with the discovery of metallic alien metal planted in his body.

Roger is thrust onto a path he never dreamed his life would ever take as one of the chosen few to start something that philosophers and spiritualists have discussed for centuries; the Ascension of humanity.

Only this isn't how the human race's next level of evolution was supposed to happen, and nor did Roger think he was the guy that would pull it off.

Toss in a guardian angel, alien hunters and Roger soon begins to realize his life's perfection ends with the understanding that memories are the illusion to which reality is draped and all is rarely as it seems in the journeys of a soul's growth. Especially when he doesn't even know how to spell chakra, let alone deal with having to master the seven levels in order to attain ascension.

Nor can time, as he knows it, be measured in heartbeats or lifespans and a heavy price must be exacted in order to stand in the gateway between memory and knowing, reality and illusion.

Especially when that effort means stopping those who would doom humanity's next phase of evolution.

Short Story Anthology Volume One:

What I'd Say To Buddha If I Met Him In The Pub

(Includes Sylvia's Sun-catchers, voted #1 by the readers in Rejected Manuscripts Anthology)

Enter the literary world of Frank Talaber, Canada's Foremost Off-Beat Author

A natural storyteller, whose compelling thoughts are freed from the depths of the heart and the subconscious before being poured onto the page.

Literature written beyond the realms of genre he is known to grab readers; kicking, screaming, laughing or crying, and drag them into his novels.

Short Story Anthology Volume Two:

What I'd Say To Einstein If I met Him On The Dance Floor

(Includes Sylvia's Sun-catchers, voted #1 by the readers in Rejected Manuscripts Anthology)

Enter the literary world of Frank Talaber, Canada's Foremost Off-Beat Author

A natural storyteller, whose compelling thoughts are freed from the depths of the heart and the subconscious before being poured onto the page.

Literature written beyond the realms of genre he is known to grab readers; kicking, screaming, laughing or crying, and drag them into his novels.

Short Story Anthology Volume Three: What I'd Say To Agatha Christie If I Met Her In The Knitting Circle (Soon To Be Released).

Social Media Links

Visit Frank Talaber's Published Author page on Facebook at:
https://www.facebook.com/FrankTalaber/
(If you want to join his fans' newsletter to hear about his latest ventures, send him a request to his email at twosoulmates@shaw.ca

Website:
https://franktalaberpublishedauthor.wordpress.com/

Facebook Short Stories Page:
https://www.facebook.com/franktalaberpublishedauthor/

Twitter:
@FrankTalaber https://about.me/ftalaber

Linkedin:
https://www.linkedin.com/feed/

My novels on Amazon.

https://www.amazon.com/stores/Frank-Talaber/author/B00UC407R0

https://www.amazon.ca/Autumns-Summer-Felicity-Talisman/dp/1738658376

My Youtube Channel.

https://www.youtube.com/channel/UCx5ki4gpdokN-9KAIZzu53w

Instagram

https://www.instagram.com/franktalaber

Goodreads

https://www.goodreads.com/author/show/8092362.Frank_Talaber

Ebooks on Smashwords:

https://www.smashwords.com/profile/view/Frank38

Instagram

https://www.instagram.com/franktalaber58

tictoc

https://www.tiktok.com/@franktalaber

Ko-gi Funding Page

https://ko-fi.com/franktalaber?ref=onboarding_email_founderwelcome

Medium Site

https://medium.com/we-paw-bloggers/the-doctor-to-the-rescue-byline-frank-talaber-b5aa29203065

Manufactured by Amazon.ca
Bolton, ON

40815145R00227